THE SECRETS
OF THE
Castle

THE SECRETS
OF THE
Castle

THUNDER AND LIGHTNING SERIES · BOOK 1

AARON M. ZOOK, JR.

Bold Vision Books
PO Box 2011
Friendswood, Texas 77549

ISBN: 9780991284269

Library of Congress Catalog Card Number: 2011929587

Printed in the United States of America.

**Bold Vision Books
PO Box 2011 Friendswood,
Texas 77549**

Unless otherwise noted, all Scriptures are taken from the *New American Standard Bible*, © 1960, 1963, 1968, 1971, 1972, 1973, 1975, 1977,1995 by The Lockman Foundation. Used by permission.

Previsouly published by WinePress Publishing

I dedicate this book to my two sons, Jeremiah and Michael. Their zest for life, adventurous natures, and desire to investigate the world around them inspired the creation of this Thunder and Lightning story and the upcoming sequels. May God bless them and their families with the same joy I find in them.

CONTENTS

Chapter 1

DRIVING
DISASTER

I fumed inside. As an explorer and adventurer I craved action. But the splatter of raindrops on the windshield followed by moments of thin sunshine warming the steamy road we traveled promised another boring vacation. Bound by a seatbelt for hours on end, I dozed from unwelcome inactivity until I got my wish—sort of.

Mom screamed as our van slid sideways down the four lane road and Dad yelled, "Hang on!" He struggled to gain control of the steering wheel, but the van swung into the passing lane on our side of the German Autobahn. A shrill car horn blasted. I clapped my hands over my ears. A quiver of fear ran through my body when I glanced out the window.

"The guardrail," I cried out.

"Gabe, quiet," Mom silenced me.

I strained against my seatbelt and clenched Dad's headrest with sweaty hands. My eyes felt like they were popping out of my head. *We're out of control.* I pictured metal shrieking against metal as we impacted the guardrail. I envisioned glass shattering in my face and blood pouring out of my punctured body. *That's not gonna happen to me.* I set my jaw and stiffened my arms in a brace position, ready to duck if the windows got smashed. Our van jerked back and forth across the roadway. We sped toward the metal barrier in the highway's center. The scene burned into my mind.

Mom, face pale, pushed her hands against the front dash.

"Hold on, Thunder," my older brother, Alex, shouted. He wedged his dog between captain-style seats. Alex clutched his dog's neck and pushed his knees against Mom's seat.

I dropped one hand's death grip on Dad's headrest and pulled my dog, Lightning, off the floor and held him tightly to my chest.

At the last instant, Dad swerved away from the guardrail. The sudden move slammed my cheek against the window. Sharp pain jarred my senses to full alert. I tasted blood as I saw gray metal rails flash within inches of my eyes before we zigzagged away from the highway center and toward the thirty-foot drop-off on the Autobahn's edge. *We'll be tossed around like rag dolls if we go over the cliff.* I jammed my feet against a wall panel and Dad's seat, teeth locked down tight. Backpacks lying on the rear bench seat smashed against the window behind me then flew over to the other side. I smelled burning rubber and heard the sound of Dad pumping the brakes. My heart jumped into my throat as we rocketed toward the edge of the roadway. *Dad ... don't wreck!* My muscles screamed from the tension.

Horn blaring, a gray Mercedes sliced the air next to my window, splitting the gap between the guardrail and us. I jumped at the sound and lost my grip on Dad's headrest. My gut churned. I bit back the stinging in my throat, gulping intensely to keep my breakfast where it belonged.

Dad jerked the steering wheel left to keep us on the roadway while swerving to avoid cars darting around us. My seatbelt cut hard into my chest, and pulled my body to the right toward Alex and Thunder. A red Porsche followed by a gray-green Volkswagen slipped past us. Muscling the steering wheel, Dad battled our van to a stop on the shoulder of the road.

I zoned out, aching all over. *We made it. I'm alive.* Pulse racing, my mind went in every direction at once. *Safe. Cheek pain. Blood taste.* When my eyes focused again, I pulled my legs up to my chest, hugged Lightning close, and ran my fingers along my teeth on the left side. They came out a little red. I wiped them on a tissue. Lightning went into a frenzy of licking my cheeks and nose, but I didn't care. Other than my cheek and mouth, everything seemed to work fine as I scrambled out of my seatbelt and stuck my head between the front seats.

Sweat rolling down his cheeks, Dad seemed frozen for a moment. Then he loosened up and looked at Mom. His shoulders pressed into his seat and he let out a big breath of air, slapping the steering wheel.

"Is everyone alright?" Mom asked, twisting around to check. She hugged me, then pushed me back into my seat. She inspected each of us for broken bones and cuts. "Gabe, why are you rubbing your face?"

I explained what had happened. "My cheek's sore. I could have a broken cheek bone." I opened and closed my jaw a couple of times. My fingers were tingling.

"I'm fine," said Alex.

I looked at my fourteen-year-old brother. His face was tight and his lips pinched. Always the rock-solid, unexcitable boy with common sense and steady nerves, he was completely my opposite. He stroked Thunder, whom he had freed from the earlier death grip around his neck. Thunder now sat back on his haunches and watched what was happening.

Mom untangled herself from her seatbelt and moved through the gap between the front captain chairs to kneel beside us. She put her hand on my chest and bent my head sideways to look at my cheek. I showed her the blood on the tissue.

"We almost crashed. Did you see how close we came to the guardrail? Another foot to the left and we would have ..." I winced as she pressed on my cheekbone.

"I think you're going to live." She patted my knee.

"No fractured bones," Mom announced. Some color returned to her cheeks. Her voice was less shrill and she had slowed down a bit. She turned to Alex and put her hand on his chest.

"Both of your hearts are racing," she said.

"Let's go out and inspect the damage," Dad said as he opened his door and slid his feet to solid ground. Mom opened the side door and jumped out.

"Boys, stay inside with the dogs," Dad said.

I climbed into the driver's seat and leaned my head out the window to hear my parents talk as cars flowed by. An unexpected shiver ran through me. The cool air that flowed in through the window on this partly sunny day didn't cause the shakes. It was visions of mangled wreckage with our bodies lying crushed underneath which kept crowding into my brain. The traffic steering around our candy-apple red home-on-wheels distracted me until Dad spoke.

"That left front tire looks like it blew out," Dad said, looking up from the ruined mess.

"We put on new tires before we left Texas to come to Germany," Mom rubbed her furrowed forehead. "They're speed rated for the Autobahn."

As they talked, a German Polizei's green and white sedan pulled up in front of the van. Two men wearing tan and green uniforms got out and walked over to Mom and Dad. After brief introductions, Dad explained what had happened. Both policemen squatted down to examine the tire.

The short, older cop with a mustache stood up. "Mr. Zanadu, we did not see any oil or liquid spill on the road near the skid marks of your tires. The road was slightly wet from an earlier rain. There also weren't any sharp objects that might have cut your tire. Because these are new tires, that means someone must have intentionally slashed your tire to make it fail at highway speeds." Crouching next to the tire, he pointed out the evidence to Dad. "Where do you normally park your vehicle?"

"We keep it in a locked parking garage or on the Army base where I work."

The shorter cop tapped his mustache. "Maybe a criminal bypassed the security system in the parking garage."

The second policeman nodded in agreement. "Do you need any assistance?"

"No," Dad said. "I can put on the spare tire. We're only a few kilometers from the Esso station. I can buy a new tire there."

"Good," the older guy said. "My partner will call ahead to ensure they have the right size. Who is with you?" He opened a notebook and moved closer to Dad. The young, black-haired man went back to the Polizei car to make a call.

"This is my family," Dad said, pointing to each of us. "You've met my wife, Rachael. In the van are my two sons, fourteen-year-old Alexander and twelve-year-old Gabriel."

"And what do you do?"

"I'm a Major in the United States Army."

"Ah, I see." The policeman smoothed his gray hair back over his head. "You and your family must be careful. Are you sure there is not another reason for an attack? Something you do at work?"

Dad looked at the ground, his face tightening for a second. He kept his answer simple. "I work for military intelligence, but I can't talk about my activities. You understand."

Hmmm. On a phone call he got from work during breakfast, didn't he make a whispered comment—something about suspects—two young men who rode motorcycles? When I had asked him what was going on, he had told me not to worry.

"Alright," the policeman said. "I understand. These questions are for my report." He closed his notebook, checking the other tires for tampering. He didn't find anything wrong. He walked back to his police car.

"The Esso station has the tires you need," said the younger cop as he rejoined Mom and Dad. As the cop with the mustache came back, the younger one excused himself. Mom said goodbye and climbed into the van. I stayed in the driver's seat to catch more of Dad's talk with the cop.

"Mr. Zanadu," the policeman said, "you are not going to like what I have to say."

Dad nodded his head. "Go on."

The policeman noticed I was listening. He grabbed Dad by the elbow and moved him further away.

It was hard, but by closing my eyes, concentrating, and ignoring the sounds of cars and trucks zipping past us, I could hear them.

The cop continued. "This is a tense time in Germany. The Berlin Wall may fall this year as we work to reunify East and West Germany by the end of next year, 1990. This political tension has increased the activity of extremists, especially against American military members, in order for them to get greater news coverage."

"Okay," Dad said. "Is there anything else?"

My heart went cold at what I heard next.

"Mr. Zanadu, someone may want you and your family dead."

Chapter 2

THE THREAT

Did I hear that right? Someone's trying to kill us?

The mustached cop said a few more things, but I didn't hear anything. I swallowed hard a few times and stared at the traffic. Out of the corner of my eye, I saw Dad say goodbye to the cops, pivot, and stride back to the van. The policemen got into their car and drove away.

Twenty minutes later, Dad had finished changing the tire and we were back on the road, moving a bit slower.

"Dad, who did this to us?" Alex asked as we poked along.

"I don't know," he said, patting the steering wheel with his hand and looking away into the distance. "I checked the tires yesterday. They were fine. The vandals must have done this last night or while we were loading the van when I was talking to Herr Klaus."

That didn't make sense to me. "If it happened while we loaded the van and you talked with the landlord, the vandals would have to be invisible. Alex and I were racing up and down the stairs with all our stuff during that time."

"Honey, you can't see everything," Mom stroked Dad's right arm, leaning toward him, her face still a bit pale. She changed the subject. "I'm glad you kept us on this side of the Autobahn and safe. Thank God we didn't get hit by all the traffic around us."

"What did the policeman mean about a criminal getting into our garage?" I asked. "And why did he say someone wants us dead?"

Mom's eyes darted over to Dad and her eyebrows arched in a questioning fashion.

Dad grew silent for a moment, then spoke. "Our family needs to be careful. Be on the lookout for strange events. I am working on a special project, but it shouldn't affect any of you." Dad looked at Mom. He shook his head warning her not to talk about it right now.

Be careful? Look out for strange things? Like someone slicing our tires when we weren't around? Imagine if we had wrecked. Our van would be on its side with our mangled bodies lying all around. I shuddered.

Dad pulled into an Esso station to fill up the tank and get a new tire.

"Bathroom break," Mom said. "Boys, take the dogs for a short walk while we wait to see how long the repairs will take."

Glad to have the break, I jumped out of the van. The 'Go-Mobile.' In Germany, we were always going someplace to sightsee. We took Thunder and Lightning on leashes to a large grassy area.

Thunder, a humongous mixed-breed of Great Dane and Greater Swiss Mountain Dog, stretched his seventy-five pound muscular body. At a year old, his bull-sized neck strained against Alex's leash.

Alex yanked back. "Thunder, sit."

Tail wagging, the jet-black giant obeyed.

Lightning danced around my feet, jumping into the air. Even at eleven months, he pranced like a pup. Bouncing. Hopping. Racing. Leaping. He never stopped. His mix of Shih-Tzu and Toy Whippet backgrounds made him as fast as a cheetah. With red-gold long hair streaming behind him, his fifteen-pound body could cover any distance like a ball of fire.

Once on the grass, we took the leashes off the dogs and watched them sniff around the area.

My stomach knotted up. "Someone's out to kill us," I said to Alex.

"Don't be crazy," Alex said. "We don't know why this happened. Could've been a prank. Don't get all worked up. It's over. And I don't want to think about it. Let's talk about something else."

Talk about something else? I don't think so. We could all be lying on the highway, bleeding to death. But if I say that, he'll think I'm a baby.

"Okay. I'm glad Dad found out the Schultzes will join us on vacation. Pete and I will have a blast." Peter was my best German friend.

"Yeah. We'll have a lot more fun with them along."

"Pete's great. But not Jenna," I said. *Girls! Who needs them?* Jenna was a pain, always thinking she was so smart and bossing me around. She did like to hang around Alex a lot, like she had a crush on him. I snickered, "I bet you're glad Jenna's coming along. She's a nice girlfriend for you."

"She is NOT my girlfriend," he hissed through his teeth.

He lunged at me. I scrambled away from him, dodging and darting back and forth. The dogs joined in the fun. Alex gave up when Dad's whistle caught our attention. He waved us to come on back. Dogs in tow, we arrived to hear him say, "I spoke with the mechanic. He needs an hour to put on a new tire. We won't reach the castle until sometime after lunch. We'll stop along the way to eat at a town called Kaufering."

"Boys, we can use this time to do some home-school activities," Mom chimed in. "Get your backpacks from the van."

"But we're on vacation," I folded my arms and pushed out my lower lip.

"Read one of your books, look through your castle study guides, or write a report about our adventure." Mom said, pointing to the nearby grassy area. "You can sit over on that picnic table."

Alex shouldered his backpack, strode to the table, pulled out a book, and started reading. I slung my pack on, put my hands in my pockets and shuffled to the side of the table opposite Alex. I kicked a few stones against the curb on my way. *I'd rather run than do schoolwork.* Because we were going to see a castle on vacation,

I pulled out the information on castles I had in my backpack. I ignored the ragged edges where Thunder and Lightning had tussled with the homework folder last night, throwing my papers everywhere. I put the papers in order, glancing at all the castles we could see in Germany and dreamt about exploring underground caves and tunnels. I stopped and studied Neuschwanstein castle, my favorite. It had square and round towers, winding staircases, and at least four levels. I even had an engineer's map I had found in a German library. It showed an underground tunnel between Neuschwanstein and nearby Hohenschwangau castle. When I showed Dad, he laughed and said the map was a hoax; the tunnel was only a legend. *But it looks real to me. Maybe he's wrong. This map might help me discover that mysterious tunnel.*

I needed a bathroom break. I left Lightning at the table and raced to the building. As I rounded the corner, I heard Mom's and Dad's voices in heated conversation on the other side of the garage bay. I stopped, straining to hear over the clang of a hammer on metal, fans humming in the work area, and engines revved up to full power.

"What do you mean the policeman said someone wanted us dead? And why didn't you tell me?" Mom waved her arms wildly in the air.

"Hon, he may be …"

"Do you know what's going on?" she leaned forward. Her hand flew to her hip and she made slashing gestures with the other hand. "I've told you time after time, I don't like your dangerous job. You're gone long hours. You leave for weeks on end. And now we might get killed. This is about your job, isn't it?"

Dad stiffened his posture, took a step back, and shoved his hands in his pockets. "I'm trying to tell you what this might be about. I have no assurance …"

"Right," Mom slammed her open hand on the wall. "No assurance. I can't take this. I knew you were in danger, but now the whole family could get hurt. What are you going to do about it?" Her cheeks were glistening with shiny wetness.

"Honey, let me finish." Dad spread his arms wide. "I don't have any control in this incident and I don't know that the policeman was right. I'll check the car better in the future and be more aware of what's around us. My boss gave no indication we would be under a death threat. I'll check back with him. The only information I have is about two young hoodlums who have joined a gang or criminal organization. And I am working on a Top Secret project, but ..." Dad spotted me and stopped.

"Going to the bathroom," I pointed and raced into the safety of the tiny room. I hadn't seen Mom upset like that since Dad went away for three months. When I jogged back to the picnic table, they weren't around the garage area. Swirling thoughts of gangs and secret projects kept my mind off of castles as I settled on the picnic table bench.

"Time to go." Mom tromped through the grass towards us, puffy eyes the only sign she had been crying. "Schoolwork time is over."

We resettled ourselves in the Go-Mobile and continued driving south. After stuffing the latest schoolwork inside my backpack, I played with my Gameboy.

I was in another world when Alex's fist slammed the top of my right thigh.

Chapter 3

STRIKE ONE

"Oww," I said, grabbing my leg. "What'd you do that for?" I glared at him and swung my right arm to thump him on the chest, but he blocked me.

"Serves you right for saying earlier that I have a crush on Jenna."

"What's the matter? Is the truth a problem?"

"Boys, stop it!" Dad's eyes and creased forehead in the rearview mirror let us know he was serious.

That stopped the action. I gave Lightning a quick stroke on the neck as he leaned on the armrest to look out the left window. Rubbing my leg, I looked daggers at Alex. *You're going to get it!* Dad interrupted my thoughts and changed the subject.

"Since you two have lots of energy to burn, let's review your homework." He quizzed us on our home-schooling projects for an hour, before pulling off the road. "Here we are. This is Kaufering."

As soon as the van stopped, Alex slammed open the side door, undid his seatbelt, and launched himself out of the van. I followed, jumping over his seat, and beating Thunder and Lightning out of the door. I bumped into Alex getting out of the van.

"Watch it!" he said, and shoved me so hard I rolled in the green grass and soft pine needles. Thunder and Lightning leaped out next. I chased Alex to the nearest picnic table with dogs trailing behind. *Freedom!* I loved running around.

Mom called us back just as I tackled Alex. "Boys, come here and unload the van for lunch." Foiled at getting back at Alex, I trotted over to help Mom.

"Here," she said, "put the picnic tablecloth on the ground. I want to sit next to the grass and flowers. After you spread the cloth, go play with the dogs until lunch is ready."

"Okay." I nodded and launched into action. While we unloaded things, Thunder and Lightning sprinted around the Go-Mobile and into the field, chasing each other back and forth, tumbling over each other, and racing back to us.

The weather had warmed up since breakfast. I didn't need a jacket. A few puffy, white clouds hung in the sky's brilliant blue background. The sun's yellow rays cast strong shadows of the nearby trees on the green carpet of newly-mown grass and on the picnic table. Pine trees, elms, and oaks surrounded our clearing, which was about a football field in length. Some brown leaves had fallen on the ground, but the leaves on the elm and oak trees were changing colors to yellow, orange, and red. The calm, greenish-colored Lech River flowed sixty feet away, paralleling our picnic area.

"Lightning, here I come." I tore out after him. I raced past Mom's red-checkered tablecloth and the picnic tables to get closer to the river. For the next ten minutes, Alex and I sprinted after each other and our dogs. I'm sure as we flashed back and forth, we looked like a laughing, falling, pouncing, wrestling madhouse. At least, that's how I felt.

"Boys, lunch is ready," Mom said above the din.

The dogs, Alex, and I rolled around together and tangled into a pile as we grappled in the grass.

"Just a minute," Alex called back to Mom.

Thunder growled as he jerked away from the pile with a stick clenched in his jaws.

Alex growled back at him. His shoulders tensed. Crouching, he grabbed the stick. He leaned back, straining to pull it out of Thunder's mouth. But the dog's powerful jaws and muscular body didn't give in. His paws, larger than Alex's fists, dug into the ground. He ripped the broken branch away from Alex.

"Let go, Thunder," Alex said. He swung one arm around Thunder's neck to separate the thick branch from his mouth, but Thunder wiggled his powerful head out of Alex's grip.

I'll get Thunder to drop that stick. I distracted him. "Lightning, catch," I said as I threw a tennis ball high in the air past Alex and Thunder.

Looking like a long-haired fox, Lightning flashed through Thunder's feet to get the bouncing ball. Thunder immediately let go of the stick to chase Lightning. Alex slammed back into a tree, sprawling onto the grass on his back.

Alex bellowed, "Come back here, Thunder."

"Thunder, leave Lightning alone," I said. "Lightning, get the ball."

Lightning caught the ball and eyed Thunder as he charged. Lightning zoomed down the bank of the river towards the water.

"Lightning, no. Not that way," I said, waving my hands as I ran towards the river.

"Boys, stay out of that water. For the second time, come to lunch," Mom said in a loud voice. She motioned for us to come back.

Mom's warning came at a good time for us, but it was too late for Thunder. Lightning made an immediate left turn at the water's edge, but Thunder's bigger size and weight kept him sliding forward through the mud, taking him right into the water. His legs churned frantically to stop the inevitable impact. *Sploosh!* Water flew in every direction.

I bent my knees, laughing until I had to hold my sides. "That's great," I choked out. *You dumb dog. Now you'll be in a heap of trouble.*

Thunder sat in a muddy pool of water up to his chest. His ears drooped as he looked back at Alex.

I kept chuckling at Thunder's predicament. Lightning trotted back to me with the ball in his mouth, head held high. "You look like the winner." I congratulated my fleet-footed friend and rubbed his head in a circular motion. *My dog is smarter.*

"Alexander, get your dog out of that water and cleaned up before we leave," Dad said as he walked toward us. "But first, get up here for lunch right now. Your mother called both of you boys twice and we are still waiting for you. You're both at strike one!"

"But Dad," I protested. "It's Alex and Thunder's fault, not mine. Lightning and I didn't do anything wrong."

Arguing didn't work. I was still in trouble and I was ticked off. *They never listen to my side of the story. It wasn't my fault. We were just playing and Thunder couldn't stay out of the water. He's not my dog.* I slammed my feet into the ground striding back to the tablecloth. I made myself cool down on the way. *At least strike one is just the first warning. We still have two more strikes before we're kaput. Done for.*

Alex said, "Thunder, you swim in the river over to those rocks downstream. Then come out of the water where there isn't any mud and shake off."

Alex and I had trained with Dad and our dogs, teaching them key words for obedience. Both dogs were smart. They did well most of the time. The key words Alex used for Thunder were "swim, rocks, shake off."

While Thunder followed his instructions, the rest of us gathered at the tablecloth to eat lunch. I peeked while Dad said the usual prayers to bless the food and watched Thunder swim twenty yards downriver. After Dad finished praying, I munched on a peanut butter and honey sandwich and some chips as I tracked Thunder making his way out of the clear water.

Thunder clambered out onto the rocks, then he paused, staring at us and licking his chops.

Here we go, I thought. *Looks like something broke his train of thought. He's probably thinking "Swim, rock, FOOD!"*

Thunder leapt from the rock, galloped across the grass like a small Shetland pony, and slid into the left side of the tablecloth near the dog food bowl. His wet body knocked a few food dishes around, but he didn't seem to notice. He flopped his rear end on the ground, chowed down on his food, and drank his water.

Alex's eyebrows narrowed. He wrinkled his nose and scrunched his face into a disapproving frown, and said, "Thunder, you forgot something."

Thunder stopped eating and looked straight at Alex.

"I didn't say 'Swim, rock, FOOD.' What was the third command?"

Thunder barked as he stood up. River water dripped off his coat like raindrops. His body wiggled as he remembered the last command.

Alex cried out, "Duck!"

Too late. Thunder jumped further onto the tablecloth, showering us with water.

"Stop, stop!" we all yelled in unison. Mom and Dad threw their hands up to shelter their faces, but I threw myself on the ground and rolled left to get out of the spray. I leaped to my feet as Mom and Dad stood up, each of us wiping off our faces and clothes. Thunder had twisted the tablecloth, spilling and mixing the food containers. Then he tilted his head while looking at Alex, showing his confusion.

Exciting. That felt kind of good in the sunshine.

Dad's eyes fixed on Alex. With hands on his hips, disappointment poured out without a word being said. Finally, he pointed to a pine tree about fifteen feet away. "Alex, get your dog over to that tree. He can finish shaking off there. Go! Now!"

"And you will have to help clean up this mess when you get back," Mom said. "There are some extra towels for the dogs in the back of the van. Make sure Thunder is completely dry. Those dogs smell like dirty laundry when they're wet."

I leaned my head back and winked at Alex, hiding my smiling lips. *Back at you, brother. Serves you right for hitting me earlier. Now you've gotten in trouble twice. I'm looking pretty good.*

Mom and Dad checked out the damage. Without comment, they started packing things up.

No talking? That's not good. No talking usually meant big trouble.

Alex glared at me a couple of times while furiously towel-drying Thunder.

I helped load the Go-Mobile and soon we were back on the road—a two-lane country road with less traffic and slightly slower speeds. After ten minutes of rocky silence, Mom and Dad started talking again.

"I guess Thunder's river-water shower woke us all up!" Dad chuckled a bit. "The water was cool and refreshing."

"My clothes don't show any stains. I guess we're in good shape," Mom said.

I tilted my seat back, smiling as I remembered the trouble Alex had gotten into with Thunder. *Better him than me. He always gets me in trouble.* I looked over at Alex, who ran his finger over his throat in a slashing sign. Then he pointed back at me. I didn't care as long as I wasn't in trouble.

Ignoring him, I said, "How much longer till we get there?"

"Looks like 3:30 P.M.," Mom answered from her pile of maps.

I moaned inside. *Another two and a half hours in the van? This castle had better be pretty good or I'm gonna die from boredom.*

Suddenly, I heard a quick buzz as a single motorcycle zipped past, traveling a lot faster than we were. He wove in and out of traffic, slowing down as though waiting for us to catch up. Then he made a U-turn and flew past us in the other direction.

I twisted around to see where he had gone, but couldn't track him.

Dad looked into his rearview mirror. "Here he comes again on our right side."

"Look at that wheelie." Alex swiveled halfway around. "He's going to crash into us."

Chapter 9

THE ROMANTISCHE STRASSE

The motorcycle's front wheel slammed to the pavement next to the van. Dad veered left. The bike rider slowed. I lost sight of him as we rounded a curve. Our home-on-wheels swung back into the right lane.

"Eli, we've got to report this." Mom reached across the gap between their two seats, touching his shoulder. "Let's see if there is a roadside emergency phone we can use."

The roar of motorcycles behind us cut off any answer.

"There are three of them now." I turned to see the action. Two zipped past like racers on a speed track, sliding by a black Mercedes in the oncoming traffic lane. The last motorcycle stayed on our bumper.

Thunder and Lightning barked at the windows, tracking the bike riders.

"Keep those dogs quiet," Dad said.

I grabbed Lightning. "Shhh!" Alex did the same with Thunder.

"Stop the car, honey." Mom tugged Dad's shirt.

"Can't. The biker behind us is too close."

19

The two riders in front sliced the air with wheelies side-by-side. Then they dropped their front wheels and unseated themselves, one to the right of his bike, one to the left. Leaning on their gas tanks with their hips, they each stretched out one leg and tapped the other's toe, wobbling for a split second.

A *thunk* behind me caught my attention as the third biker's front wheel tapped our rear window. Lightning sprang to our defense, yapping and snarling at the intruder. The lone biker braked and shot to our left, passing us while the guy stood on his gas tank. I pressed against the window to see better. He waved at us, sat down, then cut us off, driving only a foot or two from the front of the van. He stayed the closest to us. He ripped something out of his bike bag and threw it.

Dad angled right, but not fast enough. Brown muck splattered onto the windshield.

"What is that stuff?" Alex said while straining against his seatbelt.

"Looks like a small bag. And it smells disgusting." Dad flicked on the windshield wipers to clean off the mess.

"Wow." I held my nose and stretched myself as far forward as I could into the gap between the driver and front passenger seat. "That's wild. Their driving is insane."

"Yeah," Alex pushed me a little to the left. "Insane is right. And their present on our windshield makes me think of a cow barn that hasn't been cleaned out for months."

Then Thunder pushed his big head up under my chin and Lightning joined in by leaping on top of Dad's armrest to watch the motorcycles disappear down the road.

"Boys," Dad broke in, "those riders are very dangerous; especially on this road. Pretty scary."

Mom held her hand over her mouth, eyes beginning to get red. "If they were trying to scare us, they succeeded."

Dad pulled onto the shoulder of the road. He got out, walked to Mom's side, opened her door, and gave her a hug.

She shook for a moment, wiped her nose with a tissue, then sat down again. "We've got to report this," she pushed her hair back and sniffed.

"We will," Dad nodded. "Next town, I'll stop and call." He took out some windshield washer fluid and, while wrinkling his nose, cleaned the smelly deposit off the windshield. "That was a pretty strong odor," he said while getting us moving again. "Did anyone see those motorcyclists clearly so we can report them?"

Alex and I looked at each other and shook our heads.

"Not me," Mom said. "We sure have run into a lot of trouble on this trip." Her hands fidgeted in her lap until she pulled out her needlework to calm down.

"We sure have." Dad rubbed his forehead. "I thought this road would be a lot quieter."

I glanced out the window. "Why? What's so special about this road?"

"Highway B17 has a special name in German, the 'Romantische Strasse.' Does anyone know what that means?" Dad said.

I took a quick stab at the answer. "The Roman Road."

"You got the answer half right," Mom said without looking up from her needlework pattern chart.

"You've been in Germany a while," Dad continued. "You know 'strasse' means street. So what about that word 'romantische'? If it doesn't mean Roman, what's the translation?" He shrugged his shoulders and raised his hand.

"'Romantic,'" Alex said. "So this little road is the Romantic Street."

"Absolutely right," Dad slapped the dash.

"But why can't motorcyclists ride fast?" I leaned forward to hear the answer.

"Highway B17 is considered one of the best roads to see Germany's sights and to take relaxed, romantic trips," Mom put down her needlework, pointing out the window. "You soak in the autumn-colored trees, green pastures, livestock, and centuries-old buildings. A peaceful setting. If people want to get somewhere fast, they can use the Autobahn. On this road, people slow down to enjoy the cities, castles, and scenery. Mixing high speeds and sightseeing tourists is dangerous."

"And crazy motorcycle tricks," Dad looked over his shoulder.

"Okay," I sighed and looked away. "I got it." I pulled Lightning into my lap and sat back into my chair.

"Hon, there's a phone to call the police." Mom patted Dad's arm.

Dad turned off the road, got out, made the phone call, then pulled back into traffic.

"Alright," Dad said. "Quiet time."

Quiet time always lasted an hour. If you didn't sleep, you still had to be perfectly quiet.

Mom reclined her seat and threw a shawl over her head. Alex leaned back as well. Thunder stretched out in the gap between the second row captain's chairs and Lightning curled up in my lap.

Pressing my face closer to the window, I wanted to fly along like those motorcycle riders. The bigger bikes moved out at over a hundred miles an hour—Autobahn speeds. I daydreamed of weaving around cars, wind tearing at my leather jacket and pants—racing sportsters. I leaned into turns under a brilliant blue sky with white puffy clouds and sped past eighteen-wheelers. I did wheelies in front of my friends and made my tires smoke by spinning doughnuts in the parking lot. Endless power and control. Freedom to go where I wanted to when I wanted to. *I'm gonna buy a motorcycle when I'm older.* Decision made, I refocused on playing my Gameboy. Lightning stirred in my lap, but a few gentle strokes settled him back down. Mom, Alex, and Thunder had fallen asleep. Alex's light snoring didn't bother me. Between playing games, to pass the time, I watched for town signs. In an hour I saw Landsberg, Schongau, Peiting, and finally Steingaden. Now Lightning was asleep. I was proud of myself for keeping him quiet.

"Naptime's over." Dad's standard greeting gave us permission to talk. "Let's get out something to drink."

Mom shifted under the shawl, flipped up a corner, blinked, and stretched as the seat slowly came upright. Her head turned left and right to work out the kinks.

Alex's left hand worked behind Thunder's left ear, rubbing his fur. Alex yawned. "I'm hungry." His chair came upright as he finished speaking. "I'll get the drinks from the back." He unbuckled his seat belt and moved to the bench seat behind us where we stored a small cooler and snack bag.

I took a Capri-Sun from Alex after he handed out the drinks to everyone else.

Mom handed out plastic sandwich bags filled with our special gorp trail mix: M&M's, Rice and Wheat Chex, raisins, nuts, and dried fruit. "Do you want to know which castle we are going to?" she asked.

"Yes," Alex said.

"There's a castle whose name means 'new swan stone.' Can you figure out the name?"

I spit out as fast as I could, "Neuschwanstein!" I smiled with satisfaction as I answered first. I loved beating my older brother at something. I took the unsuspecting Lightning in my hands and bounced him up and down. "We're going to the best castle in the world." I ruffled his long hair and gave him a quick hug. I had put Neuschwanstein's pictures, info sheets, and my engineer map at the beginning of my castle folder. It was the number one castle on my "must see" wish list since we had arrived in Germany. The castle had all kinds of hidden secrets.

"Yep, we're gonna have a blast." Alex scratched his furry friend's neck just under his collar. Thunder's eyes closed as he stretched his neck further for more scratching.

I bounced as high as the seatbelt would let me. "How long till we get there, Dad?"

"Oh, we'll see Neuschwanstein from a distance today in an hour. Then we'll get some rest at our hotel. Tomorrow we'll be spending most of the day there. There is another castle we'll see while we're there also. Hohenschwangau, another of King Ludwig II's castles. You already know about the folk-legend that an underground tunnel connects the two. No one has ever tried to prove the tunnel really exists."

"Awesome." Alex smiled. "Who knows? Maybe we'll find that tunnel if we get to do some caving."

"Yeah, caving." The words automatically came out of my mouth. "Look. Even Thunder and Lightning want to get there now."

Lightning was so pumped up he leaped onto Thunder's head to see and hear better, looking out the window at the same time. I fell back in my seat and laughed. Lightning made Thunder look like a black lion with a golden-red mane, or perhaps like a crazy dog wearing a wig.

The view out of my window was of dark green mountains rising in the distance with rocky peaks on the horizon. Soon my mind became preoccupied with castle thoughts. I wanted to touch the stone walls, see the paintings, and explore Neuschwanstein's creepy dark stairways we had studied at home months ago. I shifted my body left and right, squirming in my seat as I imagined climbing up circular tower staircases or going down to the dirty, smelly basement and finding the legendary tunnel between the castles. Despite all the excitement, I also felt a sense of danger. Not only did the castle seem mysterious, there was something sinister about it. When we studied the castle, we learned that the king who built it died suddenly before he could finish the project. A few other people near the castle had vanished mysteriously since the king's death. Now, someone had tried to wipe us out on the Autobahn and scared us on our way to the castle. Was our connection with the castle jinxed like the king's and the others who had disappeared?

I shook my head.

"Are you okay, Gabe?" Alex kicked me.

"Hey, watch it." I kicked him back. I reached behind me to get my backpack off the bench seat. I wanted to pull out my castle papers again. But something was wrong. The zipper was already open. When I looked inside, the castle file was missing.

Chapter 5

CASTLE IN
THE DISTANCE

I backhanded Alex's shoulder. "What did you do with my stuff?"

"Nothing, nitwit." Alex crossed his arms and set his jaw.

"You're the only one who could have opened my backpack."

"Really?" Alex raised his eyebrows and tilted his head like he was a king and I was a lowly subject. "What about the dogs?"

"Boys, settle down," Mom turned to look at us. "What are you arguing about now?"

"Alex took my castle folder that had my Neuschwanstein papers."

"Okay, okay," Alex pulled the tabbed file from under his seat. "I was only borrowing it—to make some drawings."

"Enough." Mom held her right hand in the air like a stop sign. As she shifted position to see us better, her lips formed a straight, tight line.

"You two need to learn to share."

She made Alex apologize to me and I had to let him use my castle papers for the drawings he wanted to do. I didn't want to look at Alex. I turned my head, taking in the scenery outside the window.

"Neuschwanstein ahead. Ten o'clock position," Dad announced half an hour later.

I leaned toward the front of the van. The long plain we drove through with its open fields and German countryside buildings was at the base of the hills. Jutting out of a forest of green pines and trees of various shades of red, orange, and brown, the castle of my dreams stood alone on a steep hillside. Its white stones, with square and round towers topped by black-shingled cones stood in contrast to the fall colors below. Parts of the tower stones were a golden hue and the lower castle entrance was made of red brick. The castle claimed my full attention. I dropped my backpack and leaned against the window.

"There's Hohenschwangau," Alex pointed a little more to the right. "They're both on steep, rocky hills surrounded by thick German forest. I bet that's for security."

Bummer. Alex was at it again. He insisted on analyzing everything in detail, which spoiled the fun of sightseeing. Sometimes he talked like an engineer. I blocked him out and stared at the two castles thrusting into the sky.

Hohenschwangau was quite different from Neuschwanstein. The walls were yellow-gold bricks with red rooftops on most of the buildings. The towers and walls were tipped with red tiles, which stood out in the distance, even though it was on a much lower hill than Neuschwanstein.

"Dad, can we get out and take a picture?" I said.

"Sure, but let's make it quick. It's time to get to the gasthaus—our hotel."

The excitement for tomorrow's adventure started to build again. Dad took several quick pictures of us with Neuschwanstein on the huge hill behind us for a backdrop. Then he took some with Hohenschwangau behind us. The castles looked ancient. I could imagine knights riding into their gates.

After twenty minutes, Dad turned the van around and we drove back to Fussen to stay at the Alpenblick, our gasthaus for the night. I saw Alex writing in his notebook. I poked him. "Hey, Mr. Brains. What're the notes for?"

"None of your business, dimwit," Alex said. He checked to make sure Mom and Dad were occupied, then put his finger on his lips to silence me. He mouthed, "It's a secret."

I moved Lightning from my lap and craned my neck to see what Alex had been drawing.

Chapter 6

THIEF IN
THE NIGHT

Alex showed me a crude sketch of a castle that kind of looked like Neuschwanstein. A tunnel connected it to another castle. I could make out two small figures going into the tunnel.

Alex must be making plans for our next adventure, I thought. One I knew I could enjoy. Even with him.

"Boys," Dad's voice snapped me back to reality. "Here's the village where we'll stay at tonight." Mom put her needlework away as Dad pointed out the different restaurants and shops. We packed our backpacks.

Driving up the hill, we passed open-air restaurants, outdoor sidewalk cafes, and clothing and gift shops with awnings. All were open for business and strolling people filled the sidewalks. Up ahead, next to the cobblestone road, the Alpenblick came into sight, its balconies overflowing with plants. At the gasthaus parking lot, a silver-blue minivan with German license plates stood out.

"Gabe, did you see that?" Alex thumped me on the leg. "The Schultzes are here."

"Dad. Mom. You didn't tell us the Schultzes would stay at the same hotel with us," I said.

Mom smiled. "Honey, we didn't tell you all of the exciting things we'll be doing. We thought it would be more fun to have a few surprises."

When the van stopped, we shot out of the car like fireworks. Thunder, Lightning, Alex, and I rushed around the corner of the building and through the hand-carved wooden doorframe into the large lobby of the guesthouse. We found Jenna and Peter down one of the hallways and learned their family was staying in rooms 17 and 18. All four of us took the dogs back to the lobby to find which rooms we were going to stay in.

Dad picked up two keys at the front desk. "We are in rooms 117 and 118, on the second floor, right above the Schultz' rooms. You four kids help me move our luggage and gear to the rooms."

In ten minutes the work was done. Mom, along with Karl and Frieda Schultz, were upstairs when everyone arrived with the last bags.

"We have twenty minutes until dinner," Mom said. "You boys need to unpack."

"I don't take that long to unpack," I protested.

"No more," Dad's hand cut through the air. "Stop constantly challenging what you're told to do. We all need a break before we eat."

"I don't want a break. I want to see my friend." I motioned back toward Pete.

Dad leaned close to me and grabbed my shoulder. "If you don't straighten up now, you won't see your friend tonight and you won't eat dinner. Go to your room and unpack."

"Yes, sir." I turned toward my room, hunched my shoulders and kicked my shoes against the carpeted floor. *Mom and Dad never let me have what I want. We just arrived. How can we make plans with Peter and Jenna to explore and go caving together if we have to stay here and unpack?*

I shoved open the door into the room Alex and I were sharing. The room was clean as a whistle, except for our bags. That would change in about two seconds. As I looked around, the beige walls blended in with the highly polished, oak-colored wooden floors. The ceiling was an off-white color with a single overhead light. Two wheat-colored, stand-alone wooden closets with hand-painted woodsy scenes on their front panels stood next to two small-poster oak beds with humongous white pillows, dark-red comforters, and white sheets. Each bed was against a wall and between them was a small simple nightstand with a lamp. On one wall there was a wooden dresser with hand-carved drawer handles. The bathroom was a small European type, with an inexpensive shower, porcelain sink, and white ceramic toilet. The bathroom's door was near a sliding glass door opening onto a balcony.

"Wow," I said. "I bet this cost a lot of money. But there's no gadgets—no TV, no radio, no CD player. I won't have anything to do."

"Yeah," Alex nodded. "Did you bring your adapter for the electrical plug? You can plug in your Gameboy and play Tetris or Mario. I want to take a closer look at these pictures on the walls." He motioned to several pictures of the Bavarian towns and the Alps surrounding the town that hung over our beds.

I threw my pack on the bed and opened up my small suitcase to take out my clothes. "I'm gonna check out the real view from our balcony when I'm unpacked."

Alex opened his backpack and said, "Hey! Throw that brochure for Neuschwanstein that's on the dresser over to me."

"Get it yourself! I'm unpacking." I shot back. I was still taking things out of my backpack and putting them on my bed.

"Stop being a jerk all the time. No wonder Mom and Dad talk about how out of control you are. I was just asking for a little help." Alex shrugged his shoulders and walked over to pick up the glossy folder. "I thought we could do some planning for tomorrow. Remember the picture I was drawing?"

"Well, I'm planning for tomorrow too," I said. "I have to organize my stuff so Pete and I have everything we need when we find a cave to explore." I felt a tingle run down my spine when I said "cave," but ignored the feeling.

"You two are going caving tomorrow? Where are the caves?" Alex said. "Does Mr. Schultz know some local places to go caving?"

"Pete says there are some caves up on the mountainside, but not around here." I started counting batteries on my bed. "He said we might be able to go in the afternoon after we see the castle."

"Good idea, but I bet Mom and Dad would want me to go with you, along with Thunder and Lightning. You know … to make sure you and Pete stay safe." Alex shook his head. "You're too … what's the word … spontaneous. Let's make a plan. We'll see lots of action."

I sat down hard on my bed and turned away. Alex always had to horn in on what I had already started. He was always messing around with my way of doing things. If he was such a planner, he should have talked to me first. Even if there was a little danger, he had no right to take over the fun time I had set up with my friend.

"Don't start sulking," Alex said. "Our plans are always better when we combine them. Besides, we need both Thunder and Lightning with their search and rescue training in case something goes wrong in the cave."

"Yeah, but you're not like me and Pete. You're too cautious—too slow. We don't need more bosses. We want adventure, fast and furious."

"With Jenna and me along, as well as the dogs, we may be able to do some caving without the adults," Alex said with that king attitude of his.

The phone on my nightstand rang.

"Don't answer," Alex cautioned me. "Dad said not to answer hotel room phones unless we're expecting a call. Not answering is supposed to keep people from knowing we're here. He said it's for our protection."

I let the phone ring a few times. A shiver ran up and down my back. "My sixth sense says something's not right."

"What a sissy! You're not scared because we almost had an accident on the way here, are you?" Alex threw his pillow at me.

I ducked, lunged at him, and knocked him first onto his bed and then into the wall.

Alex's head bounced off the wall with a thud. His eyes narrowed and lips tightened. He grabbed me and bent me back over the head of the bed.

I shifted my weight, grabbed his left arm, and let myself fall over. Alex's arm stiffened, giving way at an odd angle.

"Ahh! That hurt," he yelled, then flipped over the bed on top of me. His first punch hit the top of my head.

"Don't call me a sissy." I blocked his second punch and pushed against his face with my hand, trying to bend his nose. He pulled back his head. I swung my left fist and split his lower lip.

The doorknob between the two rooms rattled.

I glanced at Alex and gulped as the door swung open.

Dad's head poked through the door's opening. "Time for din … Hey what's going on here?"

"Alex called me a sissy." I shoved my brother away.

"He deserves it. He doesn't shut up, talking about that accident." Alex stood up, wiped his lip, then got a tissue and pressed it down to stop the blood.

"I don't want to hear or see anymore fighting," Dad said. "If I do, you'll both be grounded for the rest of this trip. Let's get downstairs for dinner."

The door between the rooms shut.

"Let's go, Lightning." I rolled to my knees, popped up to my feet, straightened my shirt, and headed out the door, followed by Alex. Thunder and Lightning pushed their way out between our legs as we walked into the hallway. I turned back to close and lock our door.

In the restaurant, Peter and I sat next to each other on one side of a booth. Jenna and Alex were in the same booth on the other side. I talked with Pete for a while, catching up on sports, movies, caving, hang-gliding in the Alps, rock climbing, and other dangerous activities. Thunder and Lightning behaved well enough to go unnoticed for the entire meal. Most European restaurants allowed dogs inside, but they weren't allowed to disturb other customers.

"I like the skis, snow boots, and snow scenes on the walls," Pete said to me. "I'd have lots of fun snow-caving here."

"More danger, more fun." I pushed him sideways. "And I like the huge stone fireplace in the corner. Warming up with a cup of hot chocolate after snow-caving sounds great."

Jenna looked over at Pete and me. "I heard you two want to go caving tomorrow by yourselves. My dad may know a few places you could go, but Alex and I should come along."

"You're always trying to be the boss," I complained. "I bet our parents will let Pete and me go alone."

Pete went over to his father while I argued with Jenna. He came back smiling. "Dad is going to take us to a cave tomorrow afternoon and we don't have to take them along." He pointed his thumb at Jenna and Alex.

"All right!" I thanked him for the information and pounded him on the back. "Now we'll have fun!"

After we all said good-night in the restaurant, Alex and I ran up the stairs to our room to get ready for the next day. Alex got to the door first, reached out to unlock it, and paused.

"Hey, why are you waiting?" I asked. "We need to get to bed."

"Nitwit, the door isn't fully shut. When we came out, we were in a hurry for dinner. Did you lock this thing when we left?"

"Yes. I made sure the door was locked." My body started tensing up a bit.

"Oh, there's probably nothing wrong." Alex shook his head. "Let's see if the room is okay."

Alex slowly opened the door, leaned in, and flipped on the light switch. I slipped and bumped him into the room.

"Don't do that," Alex shoved me in the chest.

"Sorry," I spread my hands. "It was an accident."

"Give me some breathing room," Alex's hands motioned me away.

We walked into the room and looked around. Everything was in place, including the batteries I had left on the bed.

"Well, nothing out of order." Alex shook his head. "I'm probably just reacting to your idea that we're in danger going to Neuschwanstein."

"Yes, something's wrong, I can tell." I checked my backpack. My money, wallet, and I.D. card were still there. I zipped the bag shut and tossed it beside my bed, "First the phone rings for no reason, then our room door is open. Did you tell Mom and Dad about the phone?"

"Not yet," Alex shook his head. "Probably a wrong number. But like Dad told us after the tire blew out, we need to keep our eyes open for weird things." Alex grabbed the Neuschwanstein brochure and sat down on his bed to read.

I threw myself on my bed and took out my Gameboy to play a few games. I lost a few games of Tetris. Disgusted, I shut it off and, opening the sliding door, went out onto the balcony. Alex followed me out.

"Gabe," Alex said as he leaned against the flowerbox, "there's supposed to be secret passageways in the castles we're going to see tomorrow. My drawing shows us going into the tunnel between the castles."

"I know. And I have a copy of that engineering map I found stuck in a German library a few weeks ago. Dad still thinks the tunnel and map are all a myth." I broke off a flower from the window box, pulled petals off, and let them float to the ground below.

"Gabe, stop. Those flowers are to look at, not tear apart."

I finished tossing the empty stem off the balcony. "Since Dad doesn't believe in the tunnel, I'm more interested in going caving." I vowed silently that nothing would stop that from happening.

"Dad didn't say you could go yet," Alex blew out some air into the crisp, still night, looking for condensation vapor. "Only Mr. Schultz has agreed. Anyway, I've studied the brochure and there is a gorge behind the castle. There may be some caves there."

"Pete's dad told him there aren't any caves behind the castle, remember? We'll have to go someplace else to cave, maybe in the afternoon."

"Okay." Alex got quiet and went back into the warm room after a couple of minutes. I closed the sliding door, turned out the lights except for a nightlight, climbed into bed, and got under my comforter.

A crunching sound came from the direction of our balcony window. "Alex, did you hear that?" I sat up.

"No," he shook his head. "Hear what?"

"Listen!" I whispered.

The crunching sound was a little weaker.

Alex rolled to the side of his bed. I slid out of my bed, walked over, and opened the balcony door a bit to sneak a peek.

I motioned for Alex to follow.

Standing in the gravel below Mom's and Dad's balcony were two guys, maybe in their late teens or early twenties. They were trying to hide in the shadows next to the wall out of the streetlight's yellow glow. I stayed low, grabbed the cold, metal railing posts, and put my face between the bars. I could just make out a short, dark-haired guy with a mustache and a tall, light-haired guy. They were both in dark jackets and pants.

"Hey!" I yelled.

Alex leaned over me as the startled young men looked up. One stuffed what looked like a notepad into his jacket. They both ran, first along the building and then both disappeared out of sight, hidden by the other balconies. We could hear them scuffling down the dimly lit cobblestone street.

"Whoever they are, they're afraid of getting caught." My bare feet felt cold as ice from standing on the concrete balcony pad. "Time to go in," I mumbled, making my way back into the room.

"Wonder what that was all about?" Alex said as he closed and locked our balcony door. "I didn't see them do anything wrong."

"I didn't like it." I sighed and climbed back into bed. "There's something wrong here. We'll have to tell Mom and Dad."

A knock on the door between the rooms startled me.

"Hey, is everything alright over there?" Mom's voice came through the door.

I opened the door. "Not really."

Alex and I explained about the two young men. Mom glanced at Dad several times during the story.

"Honey, we need to get the police on this." She slid her arm through his.

"It's late right now. The listeners didn't do anything that we can prove and we don't know where they went. We'll have to be careful tomorrow and keep our eyes open." Dad disengaged himself from Mom's arm and put a hand on both our shoulders. "If there is any more trouble tonight, wake us up."

Alex and I nodded.

Mom gave us a kiss on our foreheads. As she and Dad closed the door between our rooms, I walked back out to the balcony window to see if anyone was there. Empty.

Padding back to bed, I yawned. Our dogs were getting ready to sleep. Lightning was on my bed and after I crawled under the comforter, he snuggled up close. Thunder's nose and head stuck out from beneath Alex's bed. Alex's hand hung over the edge, rubbing the dog's head.

"Good night, Lightning," I whispered, ruffling my tiny friend's luxurious hair in our nighttime ritual. "Tomorrow's gonna be really cool."

"Good night, Thunder," Alex said.

As my head hit the pillow for the final time, my brain wouldn't shut down just yet. *Gorgeous mountains, huge stone castles, and caving. This is going to be a blast. I can't let anything stop us from caving tomorrow.* My thoughts began to get fuzzy. *Danger in the castle tomorrow? Nah! Still ... lots of strange things keep happening ...*

I finally slid into a warm and inviting sleep.

Chapter 7

MISSING MAP

The alarm jolted me awake. *Six* A.M. I jumped out of bed and ran to the window to check the weather. Light was just beginning to show above the mountains. No clouds. Today would be perfect. I threw open the closet door to pull out clothes for the day. I hung my jacket on one of the bedposts and noticed that Alex was still lying in his bed.

"Alex, get your lazy body out of bed," I said, waiting for a reaction. No movement. I bounced closer. "Are you deaf? *Wake-up!* We're going to the castle today and I'm going caving."

Alex swatted at me with his pillow then bunched the feather-filled weapon around his head to shut me out. At the foot of my bed, Lightning yawned, stretching out his little paws and arching his back.

"At least *you* get the idea," I said to Lightning while I pulled on some long pants. I took a peek at Thunder under Alex's bed. He hadn't moved either, except to lift his head and lower it back to his paws. I threw on a light black sweater over a maroon shirt and went to the bathroom. On the way across the room, I patted

Lightning on the head, opened up the window to breathe in cool air, and grabbed my toothbrush from my suitcase.

Alex's watch alarm went off.

"Gabe, you need to quit bothering me when I'm sleeping. You know I always get up five minutes after you do." Alex talked to my back while I brushed my teeth.

"Can't you feel the air pumping you up today?" I said between brushing, gurgling, spitting, and brushing again. "The weather's unreal—another sunny day! When did you hear of two sunny days in a row in Germany? Only in Bavaria, I think. Today's gonna be blue sky, no clouds, crisp air, and adventure straight ahead."

I couldn't see Alex, but I heard a grunt in response.

"I bet the temp will get up to seventy-five degrees this afternoon," I said. "Feels like sixty-one degrees right now. Exactly what you like."

Alex always liked cooler temperatures than I did.

"That would be sixteen degrees Celsius, if you convert to metric," Alex said.

"Right, Mr. Computer." *Show-off.* He always picked odd times to go scientific on me. I finished up and left the bathroom. "I'm glad we can do this in September when the other kids are in school."

"That's one of the advantages of being home-schooled," Alex said as he slid out of bed, into his clothes, and came to replace me in the bathroom.

"Since Mom and Dad said we have to wait for them to go to breakfast, let's take Thunder and Lightning outside."

I stroked Lightning's mane, waited for Alex to get dressed, then led the way out of the hotel to a little park across the winding cobblestone street. A sliver of sun rose above the surrounding hills. As the dogs took care of business, I enjoyed seeing the sun begin to light up the Alps, which were framed by a turquoise blue sky. The crystal clear air made everything come alive; the fragrance of the flowers in the park mixed with the aroma of fresh baked pastries from a nearby local bakery. A few early breakfast shoppers and local businessmen began trickling past us on the street. Every building within eyesight had exterior wall paintings of different village scenes.

"Let's go. I'm hungry," Alex said, bringing me back to the task at hand. We cleaned up after the dogs and went back to the room.

"Man, this is gonna be great." I stretched on my bed while waiting for Mom and Dad. "The Alps are lots of fun. Remember when Dad took you and me hiking up Jenner Mountain? You know, the one where they did the Olympics?" I glanced at Alex. He wasn't really paying attention. I didn't care. I kept remembering our past Alpine adventures. Today's caving would make another great memory.

I shoved myself off the bed and went out on the balcony, turning back to say, "Alex, if Mom and Dad say you have to come caving this afternoon, you better pack some caving gear."

"Already done." Alex looked up from his bed. "Hey, do you have that map of the tunnel between the castles? I want to see it before we take the tour this morning."

I walked back into the room, opened the closet door, pulled out the first drawer, and picked up the castle folder I had stuffed in there last night before dinner. When I opened the folder, all that was inside were remnants of papers I had done for the castle unit in school. I slapped the folder shut.

"Alex, my engineer map of the tunnel is gone!"

Chapter 8

SINISTER ENCOUNTER

After I searched frantically for fifteen minutes, I sat down on my bed next to the now worthless castle folder.

"I thought you said no one took anything last night." Alex came over to look at the folder.

"I didn't look in the closet," I said. "Only in my backpack. Do you think those guys took the engineering map?"

Alex shook his head.

Mom and Dad's arrival stopped any further discussion.

"Did we interrupt something?" Dad said.

"I can't find all of my castle paperwork, especially that tunnel map." I opened the folder to show him.

"I thought you told us yesterday that the dogs had gotten into your stuff at home." Dad took the folder from my hands.

"Well, yes," I said. "But they didn't destroy the engineer's drawing. I thought I had it with me. Our door was open last night when we came back from supper, but I know I locked it before we left. Maybe someone stole the map."

"I think you might be imagining things." Mom tilted her head, nodding slightly while raising her eyebrows.

"Never mind," I said. I closed my folder and put it back in the closet. "I guess we need to get going so we can beat the crowds to the castles."

Dad grinned. "No problem with crowds today. They'll be small because most of the children are back in school. Your schoolwork today will be learning as much about these two castles as you can. We'll have to wait in line to get in, no matter what. And you'll have to listen closely. Each tour only lasts about twenty minutes. Maybe without the crowds we'll get a little extra time." Dad continued to talk as we walked downstairs for the continental breakfast.

Thunder brushed against Dad's leg and Lightning pranced in front as the leader of the pack. I rushed down the stairs first, leaving the slowpokes behind.

When I reached the breakfast room, I stared at the awesome layout of food. Along with the sliced cold cuts on a large rectangular table in front of us, there were cheeses of all types, fruits, a variety of Brotchen—a special kind of German bread—regular bread, and hot and cold eggs. A side table contained cold drinks—water, orangensaft, apfelsaft, and various other types of juices. Another table against the sidewall held cold and hot milk. Cold milk was for cereal and hot milk was for my favorite—scrumptious hot chocolate. Finally, at the end of the table were two toasters.

I immediately turned to the rest of the family coming into the restaurant.

"Mom and Dad, the Schultzes are already here, sitting right across the room. Can we sit with Pete and Jenna? Please?" I tried to hide any sense of whining, but I really wanted to short-circuit Dad's desire for family time.

Dad and Mom looked at each other.

"Honey, that's okay with us." Mom laughed. "You boys go ahead and we'll talk with the Schultzes about today's activities."

We led Thunder and Lightning around the center food table past golden beams of sunshine cascading through multi-paned windows on one side. I turned to check on Lightning. Instead of following, his head was low to the ground as he stalked a sleeping cat in the corner. With a double click of my tongue, I caught his attention. Patting my thigh, I called him to my side. Alex had to escort Thunder, holding his collar, past two German Shepherds lying by their masters' feet.

Jenna and Pete saw us walking over and waved. They got permission to move and soon we were all sitting at one booth.

I slid into the cushioned booth seat with Pete as Alex sat opposite us next to Jenna. After exchanging a couple of friendly arm punches with Pete, we picked up trays and browsed through the food choices. My first stop was the powdered chocolate and hot milk. Next I filled a plate with a bagel (toasted of course), strawberry cream cheese for the bagel, scrambled eggs, a hard boiled egg, and potatoes. I squeezed a bowl of Cheerios and cold milk on the tray. Pete went in another direction and met me at the table.

After Pete and I got back from grabbing our food, Lightning jumped between us, rubbing his head against Pete's stomach. Thunder sat next to the booth while Alex and Jenna picked out their breakfast food. Then, when Alex came back, Thunder lay down beside Alex's feet under the table.

"Mmmm," I sniffed the aroma of the hot chocolate I had made. "I love the hot chocolate here. I wonder if this is the same as the Swiss hot chocolate we got in Zurich?"

"I don't know," Pete said between mouthfuls of eggs and toast covered with orange marmalade, "but, I know I *am* hungry and this chow *is* good!"

"What are you guys doing today?" Jenna said after she had swallowed the last of her fruit and placed her spoon in the bowl. She didn't eat much.

"Today should be pretty exciting. We're going to Neuschwanstein castle. I wonder if there is a dungeon?" I hardly stopped to breathe as I ladled cream cheese onto half a bagel, took a bite, and spoke while chewing. "I heard that you can see the lake from the castle. I'll bet there are secret passages and tunnels throughout the area." I felt my eyes start to glow.

"Don't talk with food in your mouth," Jenna interrupted. "We don't do things like that in public because it's impolite. But guess what?"

I sighed. I pointed my fork at her. "Jenna, you're being a pain. What? I don't want to guess."

"Just like an impatient child." Jenna made a face, squared her shoulders and took a few seconds looking into the distance. She looked at Alex, then back at me. "We're going to ..." she started.

Pete finished his mouthful of food in time to blurt out, "... Neuschwanstein too."

"Peter!" Jenna glared at her brother.

"Jenna, ignore him." Alex calmed her down. "Tell us what your plans are."

"We're going to Neuschwanstein too." She swung her golden hair to the right for emphasis. "And, we will be going caving after we finish the tour."

"We? I thought only Pete and me were going caving?" I said.

Jenna tightened her lips and knit her eyebrows together. "Your mom and dad talked with our parents after we went to the room last night and changed the plans, so we're all going. I found out this morning. Didn't anyone tell you?" Her eyes widened and she shrugged her shoulders.

"No, no one told us," I tapped my fork on the table. I could feel the resentment start to rise.

"Don't worry about them." Pete punched me in the arm. "We'll go in first and be way ahead of them in the caves."

Good old Pete. He always looks on the bright side. Determined not to let Jenna's announcement drag me down, my talking bubbled along without room for anyone else to get into the conversation. "Okay, we'll make this fun. But I have lots of questions. Which castle are we going to first? Neuschwanstein or Hohenschwangau? When are we leaving? Will Thunder and Lightning be able to go on the tour? Does a tunnel connect the two castles?"

"Whoa! Slow down," Pete interrupted. "Tunnels? Who said there were tunnels in the castle? My dad talked to the locals, who said there aren't any caves or tunnels near the castles."

"Well, our dad said there is a local legend about a tunnel connecting Neuschwanstein to Hohenschwangau," Alex countered, nodding to the next booth where our parents sat.

"I had an engineering drawing of the tunnel between the two castles, but it's gone now." I lowered my voice, "Maybe stolen."

A sudden movement stopped the conversation. Scrambling to his feet, Lightning jumped onto the table, facing out toward the center food table.

"Lightning, get down," I said, scanning to see what had caused the disturbance.

After I turned toward the central table, Lightning used his incredible balance to jump from the table onto my left shoulder with his head braced against my neck, still pointing in the same direction. A middle-age man wearing brown khaki pants, a dress belt, and a tan dress shirt with a tie crossed the room to linger at the breakfast bar next to Mom and Dad's booth. Lightning's tail flapped back and forth and his nails dug into my shoulder.

"Lightning!" I winced, finally pulling him down and into my lap.

But Lightning didn't stay there. He leaped to the edge of the table as the man moved toward us. The man looked over Mom and Dad, the Schultzes and each of us kids with a casual glance. He seemed disinterested, but he took his time walking by.

As the man passed our table, a faint rumble came from Thunder's throat. Alex's hand reached down and petted Thunder as he whispered, "Steady."

I looked under the table. Thunder's ears stood straight up and the hair on the back of his neck had started to bristle. *Why were the dogs reacting this way?*

Peter, Jenna, and Alex talked about today's plans while my detective-eyes focused on the older man. He was about six feet tall and had long, straight black hair that was neatly cut. Clean-shaven, with steady dark eyes, a swarthy complexion, and rough, large hands, the man sat back in his chair, playing with a spoon. A suit jacket lay on the back of his seat. His long sleeve on the right side slid back for a second, revealing a large tattoo on his right wrist—the tip of a dagger. He nodded to two younger men at his table.

Something familiar about the other two guys bugged me, but my brain couldn't make the connection. Each had on a different subdued-colored shirt with dark leather motorcycle pants. Both had on biker boots. One of the young guys had blond hair and steel blue eyes. The other had dark brown hair, a mustache, and green eyes. Behind each young man's seat was a bright black and red motorcycle helmet. Out of the corner of my eye, I saw the coat rack by the door holding two really cool, black leather jackets.

Motorcyclists. Alex loved motorcycles. Maybe he would recognize the kind of bikes these guys ride. *Wonder why they're interested in us?* I chewed on my lower lip, zeroing in on the two guys to get more details, but my thoughts were cut off.

"Time to move on," Dad said, waving a hand in front of my face to get my attention.

I nodded, then turned and gulped down the last of my hot chocolate.

"Dad, should we take flashlights in case there are tunnels between the castles or caves we can go into?" I said when our family reached the doors to our rooms.

Dad smiled. "Gabe, don't get your hopes up. There aren't any real tunnels, only a legend. Your map didn't have enough detail to confirm there was a tunnel between Hohenschwangau and Neuschwanstein. However, you and Alex should bring caving flashlights and backpacks since I've agreed with Karl Schultz that all four of you can go caving this afternoon."

Before I could ask another question, Dad and Mom went into their room. Slapping my hand against my door, I shouldered it open, and flopped down on the bed. *Now Dad says my engineering map isn't a Neuschwanstein tunnel map. And the map disappeared!* I twisted toward the wall, smacking the comforter. *And Dad confirmed Alex and Jenna were going caving too.* I punched the pillow. Nothing was going right.

"Alex, did you see that middle-aged man at breakfast?" I rolled onto my back, glancing at him. He slipped his caving flashlight into his backpack. "Was he listening to what we were doing today?"

"Maybe." Alex hung a few karabiners in his belt loops. "Seemed like he and the two biker dudes were together. Did you see the tattoo on the old guy's arm? The jagged-edged dagger? And our super sensitive sleuths, T&L, sure got excited."

I rubbed my shoulder where Lightning's nails had scratched me, remembering his weird behavior. With the dogs around, we often referred to them by their initials so they wouldn't know we were talking about them. I don't think it mattered, as they both low-crawled a little closer.

"Those guys are tracking Dad for some reason."

"Nahhh!" Alex shook his head. Then he stopped packing. "Well, on second thought, maybe. Dad does work with the Army and he probably handles some secrets. And didn't he say something about motorcyclists on that phone call he got at home?"

"Our family could be under watch by someone who doesn't like us—you know—like we're under surveillance. There might be a plot of some sort."

At that moment, the sound of two different motorcycles roaring to life broke through the peaceful atmosphere. Both Alex, me, and the two dogs jumped up, ran out on the balcony, and looked to our right. Down on the cobblestone street two figures sitting on racing bikes were taking them off their kickstands.

"Those bikes are a Ducati and a BMW," Alex pointed out.

"The helmets and clothes of the riders match exactly with the biker-dudes in the restaurant." I said.

"Quick, Gabe! Get some paper to take down the license plate numbers." Alex squinted, leaning out to get a better look.

I lunged to grab some paper from my backpack, just missing Thunder.

"Looks like Mike Lima Mike Niner Niner Tree and Delta Sierra Charlie Tree Tree Four." Alex spoke quickly, using military words and numbers.

"Got it." I acknowledged. "MLM-993 and DSC-334," I repeated, using military lingo to ensure I had heard everything right. I stuck my head through the door opening. The bikers revved their bikes, then surged down the street and sped out of sight.

Alex walked back into the room and closed the balcony door. "You'd better keep that info with us, in case we need it." He went back to packing for the castle trip.

"This vacation could be a disaster if someone's watching us." I shook my head. My racing mind leapt from one question to another while I finished packing, shoving climbing ropes, karabiners, and the paper with the license plate numbers into my pack. *Were those two young men in the restaurant the ones we had seen last night? They sure looked similar. Were we being tracked? Would our castle tour be cut short by a grisly encounter in a dungeon?* Maybe I had watched too many horror movies.

Alex broke into my thoughts. "Are you ready?"

"Yep, let's go." I swung my backpack onto my shoulder, let Lightning jump on top, and followed Alex out the door as I tried to brush away my growing fears.

Chapter 9

WHISTLE WHILE
YOU WALK

We piled into the van for the short trip to the castle. Thunder pushed his nose into my space.

Shoving his face away, my foot accidently kicked Alex.

"Watch it," Alex kicked my shin hard.

Mom and Dad hadn't noticed. A punch to Alex's arm made him massage the impact area. He swung his legs left, pressed his back against the door and kicked my thigh with both feet.

"Ouch. Alex kicked me." I jerked my leg up to my chest, laying my head sideways on my knee and clenching my eyes shut.

"Alex, don't kick your brother," Dad reached behind and caught Alex's leg, squeezing to make his point. "This car isn't moving until you two make up. And Alex, you'll be doing the laundry next week."

I smiled at Alex and raised my eyebrows at the mention of the extra chores he got for next week, but the making up ritual was a pain. We both had to apologize to each other for getting into a fight, no matter who got nailed for it, and give each other a hug. Yuck! And you couldn't give a sideways shoulder hug or pat on the back. We had to get out of our seatbelts, face each other, and put both arms around each other for a full second.

"That's better," Mom said. "And keep those dogs quiet too."

Thunder and Lightning didn't want to settle down, but Alex and I made them lay still.

"Behave," I whispered into Lightning's ear while I petted him, "or we're not going anywhere."

The twenty-minute drive flew by. Dad stopped the van in Schwangau at the bottom of the slopes of the mountain so we could see Neuschwanstein in the distance again, surrounded by a beautiful sunlit pine forest. The fresh air and country smell made me want to run through the fields and wrestle with the dogs. First, of course, Dad wanted more pictures of the castles. Then, he told Alex and me to let the dogs "take care of business" one last time before we reached the castle.

"Go get 'em, Thunder!" Alex slapped his dog on the rump to help him move out swiftly. "And don't be long, we have a fun day ahead of us."

I sent Lightning out the same way.

"Alex, I can beat you to that tree at the end of the field." I tapped his elbow and took off. Alex lost ground for a few seconds, but soon drew up next to me. We reached the tree in about two minutes flat. I walked around a bit to catch my breath. "Hey Alex," I said, "what do you think about those biker dudes? I don't like them one bit."

"Gabe, don't let all this stuff get to you until we have proof," Alex said while breathing heavily, squatting, and watching the dogs. "All they did was watch us and maybe spy on us last night. You're getting spooked. Probably all the scary movies you like to watch." Alex looked at me and shook his head.

"You watch the same movies too. But—"

"Gabe, take it easy." Alex got up, walked over, and gave me a wrestling shove. "You're acting nuts, imagining things, but I'm analyzing what's happening. I don't like the way that older guy looked at us either. If Jenna and Pete were here, we could ask them what they think."

Hands on my hips, feet spread wide, I faced Alex, tightening my mouth. *Always logical Alex. Superior Alex. Stuck up Alex.* Crouching, I moved a foot forward, then lunged with a wrestling move to grab his legs, but he twisted away. Before I made another attempt, he looked at his watch, put two fingers in his mouth and whistled for both Thunder and Lightning.

Both dogs' heads came up, although Lightning was hard to see until he hopped onto a rock. They were about a football field away. They looked at Alex, then at each other, and in the blink of an eye our furry friends raced back. I had no trouble seeing Thunder, who charged forward with great speed through three-foot high weeds. On the other hand, Lightning's golden-red hair blended in with the light-brown, wheat-colored field and I could only see the high grass bend left and right as Lightning zipped towards us. Lightning's stellar speed got him to me in half the time Thunder took to cross the distance between him and Alex. Lightning was licking his right paw when Thunder arrived.

Five minutes later we were all back in the van.

"Man, there are lots of parking areas for Neuschwanstein," I said as we arrived.

"All the town's parking sections can hold up to three thousand cars." Alex read out of his brochure. "There are millions of visitors each year."

"Looks pretty empty to me," I said.

"We're early," Mom said.

"There's the Schultzes," Alex's finger jabbed to the front right as we drove in.

"Yeah," I shouted. "Let's go."

"Dad and Mom," Alex unhooked his seatbelt, "we're going to Neuschwanstein together with the Schultzes, right?"

"Yes," Dad smiled as he put his camera bag over his shoulder.

"Then we can take the dogs and meet you up at the entrance of the castle, right?" Alex made his question almost sound like a statement.

Dad glanced at Mom for a second. I guess Dad didn't get any strange looks. He nodded his approval. "Make sure you wait for us at the top of the hill," he said. "We have to buy tickets to get in together."

"Sure, Dad," we responded. We grabbed our backpacks and took off for the Schultz' van.

"The hill up to the castle is steep." Jenna nodded at the incline as we arrived. "I think our parents will take about twenty-five minutes to walk up to the top. We can get there faster."

Alex and I took the lead with Thunder and Lightning on leashes. The main path was asphalt. Packed dirt trails laced their way through the pine trees, green trailing vines, and purple, yellow, and red fall flowers. The birds chirped loudly, chasing each other from one tree to another.

"Let's move at a Volksmarch pace. Step out lively." I swung my arms faster, lifted my knees higher and dug my toes into the ground. No one else kept up with me. "Come on, everyone. An organized walk through the woods is a lot faster than we're walking."

"Gabe, we'll take the dogs up," Alex said as he caught up and reached for Lightning's leash. "Then you and Pete can run up and down the hills. Jenna and I want to walk a little slower."

"Thanks, bro!" I said, throwing Lightning's leash to Alex.

Pete and I dashed up the hill, taking the road only part of the way. We took some of the dirt trails to cut a straighter path through the pines up the hill, bypassing the curvy road's switchbacks. We stopped on the side of the hill three quarters of the way to the top. I pointed at Alex and Jenna slowly walking up and laughed at them.

I tapped Pete on the arm.

"What?" He looked back at me.

"Do you think your sister likes my brother?"

"Yeah, they're friends, so of course they like each other." Pete shrugged his shoulders as his dark brown eyes shifted from watching Alex and Jenna to looking directly at me.

"I mean something else," I said. "You know, boyfriend/girlfriend."

"That's disgusting. If they are, I don't want to know." Pete turned to look up the hill.

I sighed and sat back on the brown pine-needle carpet, propping myself up with my hands and feeling the needles press into my skin. "Okay. Let's talk about something else. My brother doesn't want to talk about it, but ..." I stopped and waited until I had Pete's attention again. "What did you think of those biker dudes and the strange guy we saw in the restaurant at breakfast?"

"They're creepy." Pete shook his head. "That one guy with the tattoo on his hand seemed to take a lot of time near our tables."

"Yeah, I wonder if they're tracking my dad."

"Why do you say that?" Pete sat down and propped himself on a tree a few feet away from me.

"Dad had a call from work that talked about suspicious people riding motorcycles." My eyes swept down the hill, noticing that Jenna and Alex had slowed down.

"Maybe they're trying to track *you*," Pete wondered out loud. He rubbed his back against the tree as though he had an itch.

"Nope, I don't think so." I tossed a pinecone down the hill. "My dad's the one in the military intelligence field. He knows lots of secrets."

"Forget about it. It's probably nothing." Pete threw a pinecone further down the hill, almost hitting one of the green painted trash baskets along the rock wall by the road.

"Hey, watch this!" I smiled at Pete. I pulled out my silent, high-pitched dog whistle. I checked to make sure I didn't see any other dogs around.

Alex and Jenna were getting near a turn.

I blew the whistle. Without warning, Thunder and Lightning began running up the hill, pulling Jenna and Alex along. As

Thunder jerked on the leash, Alex was caught off guard and took a few steps forward to keep his balance. Lightning also sprinted, but his lighter weight was easier to control and his leash kept him from going up the hill. Jenna held him firmly. Alex jerked on the leash to halt Thunder.

I blew the whistle again at the corner of the turn. Thunder tried to break free. Alex's firm hand kept that from happening, but Thunder ran around Jenna. Lightning, seeing his buddy go right, decided to go left, wrapping his leash around Alex. In five seconds, both dogs had run twice around Alex and Jenna. The leashes pulled the two of them tightly together.

I laughed and punched Pete in the shoulder, then lay on my back and laughed some more. When I sat up, Pete and I could both see Alex and Jenna facing each other, squirming to untangle themselves from the twisted mess.

"Thunder!" I heard faintly as Alex yelled at the big black brute.

Pete jabbed me in the side. "I think my sister liked that," he snickered. "We should do that again sometime."

"Sounds like fun to me." I nodded as I watched them unravel their puzzle.

There was an awkward pause for a second. Still facing each other, Jenna adjusted her blouse and Alex shook his head. Then Jenna picked up Lightning and walked up the hill with Alex and Thunder alongside.

"Quick," I tapped Pete. "Let's run to the top before they see us."

Keeping the trees between us and Jenna, Alex, and the dogs, Pete and I slipped away up the hill, breaking into a steady run until the ground became more level.

Chapter 10

NO DOGS ALLOWED

After darting up the hill, Peter and I reached the gift and fast food shops unseen by Alex and Jenna.

"I think it's going to take at least ten minutes for Alex, Jenna, and the dogs to get here." Pete huffed and puffed.

"Are you out of shape?" I asked. "You don't normally breathe that heavy."

"I haven't run in at least a month." Pete sat down on the rock wall beside the road.

"You should train with my dad," I suggested. "Dad's always trying to prepare us for anything that might happen. He says, 'Life's an ironman race. There are lots of ups and downs, so be ready mentally, physically, and emotionally to finish the race.'"

"Sounds pretty heavy to me. What's an ironman? What kind of training do you do?"

"Well, an ironman is boring stuff like unending swimming, bicycling, and running, but then Dad lets us do some pretty cool stuff, like caving, rock climbing, archery, lifting weights, and studying martial self defense."

"I think martial arts are awesome." Pete slashed down with a karate chop.

"Yeah, if you're not doing lots of other stuff. But I don't get out of shape," I taunted Pete as I shoved him and ran toward the closest fast food shop, darting between the smiling tourists.

As Alex and Jenna finished their walk up the hill and came close, I said, "Wow, that looks good."

"What looks good?" Alex glanced around.

"Lightning," I said. "Come here, boy." I ignored Alex for a moment while I gave my dog a big hug and handed him over to Pete. I pointed to my right. "See the Eisbecher stand? They serve great ice cream. I'd love some right now. I've worked up a little appetite coming up that hill."

"You're always hungry." Pete laughed. "Remember the three huge soft German pretzels you ate in nine minutes a week ago? Seemed like you had a hole in your leg."

"Those pretzels were awesome. Sweet and salty! Lots of bread covered with cinnamon sugar. Yum, yum," I grinned back.

"I think Mom and Dad will believe it's a bit too early." Alex frowned at me.

"I know it's early, but Pete and I need some food," I said, with gusto. "Besides, we could always make do with soda, *pomme frites*, or a *wurst*."

"I like German French fries too, but we may have to be satisfied with something else, like the thin metal medallions we usually buy and nail onto our walking canes," Alex said.

"Some of the designs on the medallions are towns and other scenery, but I've seen at least one with a coat of arms." Jenna nodded toward a few other shops. "Besides, a medallion will remind you of a Volksmarching event."

"That's right," said Pete. "You want to remember our German traditions like Volksmarching."

"How could I forget all the ten- and twenty-kilometer walks in the woods we've done?" I asked. "Okay," I conceded, "I'll forget food for now. Let's go check out the shops."

We walked into the first shop on the hill. The outside had blue, red, and green dresses, blouses, shirts, and pants, and brown or black leather footwear hanging under a wooden awning. A few elderly ladies rested on gnarled wooden benches by the front windows of the store. Through the windows, I saw metal medallions and crests. Twisted walking canes covered the left wall. I made a beeline through a narrow aisle, past the Bavarian crystal display, and the glass-fronted counter full of gold, silver, diamonds, pearls, jewelry, and watches. Cuckoo clocks chimed the hour as we reached our destination.

"Here's a medallion for Hohenschwangau," Pete said while browsing.

"Is there a coat of arms or a picture?" Alex asked.

"A coat of arms," Pete said.

"Here are some hat pins." I pointed to the right. "We can stick them on our German hats. This one has Neuschwanstein's coat of arms. I've seen that several times in the books."

"Hat pins are more expensive," Jenna added.

"Money!" I shook my head. "You guys are always worried about money." I jammed my hands in my pockets, walked out of the store, and over to the stone wall where Thunder and Lightning were lying down, their tongues hanging out.

Pete came over and smiled. "Looks like the dogs are out of shape too."

I shoved him in defense as Mom, Dad, Karl, and Frieda finally strolled into sight. I grabbed Pete's arm and whistled for Lightning to follow me as we went to greet them.

"Stay right here, boys." Mom motioned us a little closer. "Dad and Karl are checking our ticket times."

"I didn't bring my money from my room, Mom. Can I get an ice cream cone or a medallion or hat pin?"

Mom thought for a second. "Not now. I think we're going in soon."

Dad and Karl appeared around the front corner of the castle and signaled us up to the castle entrance.

"Go ahead," Mom said. "Frieda and I will get the others."

As Pete and I approached the gate, Pete said, "Hey, I think they're doing a concert in the castle this evening. You know, a Bavarian concert. See that sign over there?"

"Really?" I said as I looked to my left. "Oh, yeah. I see the sign. What kind of music or songs will they play that we would know?"

"They're going to be playing the Ride of the Valkyries by Wagner," Jenna said as she and Alex joined us.

"Oh, yeah, that's good!" Pete punched his fist into his other hand. "I remember that song from the American comedy about a German prisoner of war camp. Uh, *Hogan's Heroes*, I think. The Ride of the Valkyries was the German Colonel's favorite song."

Recalling Colonel Klink listening to the song, adjusting his monocle, stiffening his back, and slashing his riding crop through the air to conduct the music made me laugh. "That was a funny sitcom. That song is awesome! Powerful! Are they really playing it tonight?"

"Yes," Alex said. "There'll be lots of people coming to the concert. They might block off the music room. I'm not sure we'll get inside to see the stage and concert area."

"That's too bad." Jenna sighed. "We're going to be caving this afternoon. We'll probably miss the whole experience. I wanted to see the music room, and I really like classical music."

"Me too," Alex said.

"Well, great," I said. "If the music room isn't going to be open, let's see if there are any secret passages we can spot during the tour."

"Count me in," Pete said.

"Halt!" a gruff voice sounded from behind me.

I looked around. A chunky man in a uniform strode in our direction. He looked like a guard. I didn't stop.

The man insisted. "Halt! You two boys with the dogs."

I stopped and turned around. "Is something wrong?"

"No dogs allowed." The man wagged his finger at us. "Especially a dog this big." His finger stuck straight out toward Thunder.

No! That will kill the whole castle tour. I tried to think fast on my feet. "We have special permission," I said.

"Show me," the guard demanded.

"I don't have it on me," I said. "Alex, why don't you get Mom and Dad to straighten this out."

"Be right back," Alex said as he shot off to find Mom and Dad.

Chapter 11

SECRET PASSAGES

I looked at the ground, then glanced at the guard who had crossed his arms and straightened his back. I pushed a few pebbles with my foot and looked up. He didn't change his position or the firm set of his jaw. I hunkered down, arm around Thunder's neck, facing away from the guard. Lightning nuzzled my chin by perching on my leg. A few minutes later, Alex and Dad's voices roused me as they came back into the courtyard entry area.

"What seems to be the problem?" Dad asked the guard.

"No dogs allowed." The guard motioned to the sign with a dog's face covered by a red circle with a line through it. "Only for special cases."

I couldn't believe Thunder and Lightning weren't going to be able to see the castle. *How could we find secret passages without them?* My insides felt like Jell-O.

Dad slowly reached into his pocket and pulled out his wallet.

"These dogs are specially trained by the U.S. government for police work." Dad looked with half-closed eyes at the guard. "I am on the lookout this weekend for some suspicious German young men. If I find them, I may have to direct the dogs to chase them."

"How can I believe you?" the guard asked.

"Here is my military I.D. Card to prove I'm in the military," Dad said as he opened his wallet. "Boys, show him the dogs' certifications."

Alex and I pulled out our wallets to show Thunder and Lightning's completion cards we had received for the summer Military Police dog handler training.

The guard looked through our paperwork.

"Where is your special permission?" He seemed to sneer. "These are only general papers."

Dad nodded, then pulled out another paper. This one was written in German.

Pushing his cap back a little, the guard looked up at Dad, at us, and then at the dogs. He shrugged his shoulders.

"Alright, that's sufficient," he said as he handed Dad's papers back and let us through. "But you must keep the dogs on leashes."

When we got inside, I tugged on Dad's shirt. "Thanks for getting the dogs in. How did you do that?"

Dad pulled Alex and me aside. "What I said was the truth. In cooperation with our local German police back home, I'm looking for a few young, dangerous German men, but that's all I'll tell you now. Your dogs' training will help me catch those men if they run away."

"Wow," I shook my head.

"Dad, just let us know and we'll sic them on the bad guys." Alex rubbed Thunder's shoulders.

"Let's hope they don't need to go into action," Dad cautioned. "And by the way, not a word to your mother. I'll tell her later tonight."

"Roger that," I mumbled, working my way forward into the gaggle of people.

By the time we caught up with the tour, the guide was telling the group of about twenty people about the castle. Mom and Dad stayed close to the tour guide, but I hung back with Pete in order to spy more easily. We left the first floor, which contained a large, unfinished entryway. Some parts of the wall were open. Gray cinder block and tan brick that formed the inside of the wall were visible right next to a finished part of the wall that used fake marble. The guide said the imitation marble finish was more expensive than using real marble. Plain walls and bare floors created echoes as we talked and walked around. Sheetrock painted in a tan color covered the walls not finished in imitation marble. Fake light gray marble with black flecks throughout covered the banisters going up to the next floor. Passing through the entryway, we went up a square, narrow rock wall staircase to the third floor landing, which gave access to the king's apartments.

I felt a tap on my shoulder. Alex.

"What?" I jerked away. "You're bothering me. We're on a tour and I want to listen."

"Make sure Lightning doesn't do anything crazy," Alex warned. "I've already had a little talk with Thunder."

"Crazy? Like what?" I said sarcastically. "Like jumping on the king's bed and going to sleep?" I snorted. "I know what to do. I'll tell him to keep quiet and stay by my side."

"Okay," Alex said. "We don't want to get in trouble."

"I know, already!" I hissed through my teeth and moved to the other side of the landing next to Pete. Even with our warnings to the dogs, both Thunder and Lightning tugged on their leashes to sniff everywhere.

I walked through the next doorway and heard the tour guide's lilting voice.

"We are now in the king's apartments." The guide made a sweeping motion to the ceiling and around the room. "Notice the vaulted ceilings with fresco paintings and marble throughout. A medieval legend was painted on the walls of the room ..."

I didn't hear the next sentence. I realized I had let go of Lightning's leash. I scanned the room for ten seconds. His reddish-blond tail stuck out of an open door of a twelve-foot long, five-foot deep rosewood wardrobe engraved with King Ludwig II's crest. No one seemed to notice. Not wanting to attract attention, I grabbed

Pete's arm and motioned for him to be silent. I silently mouthed the words, "I'll follow in a second." I placed my hand under my chin, crossed an arm over my chest, then ambled around the room, peering intently at pictures and carvings. I was acting like a studious young man as I worked my way over to Lightning.

Just as I reached the fourth door of the closet, his tail disappeared completely. When the tour guide went into the next room, she began speaking and the crowd followed, leaving me all alone. I slid into the far right door of the wardrobe only to find it empty, except for clothing that might be from the 1800s.

I let my eyes adjust to the dark red interior. Lightning's sniffing sounds came from the left corner of the wardrobe. As I pushed through the clothing, the darkness began to fade. Light flowed through an open narrow door at the back corner of the cupboard. As I peered through the opening, Lightning came into sight. He was lightly trotting down a circular stairway. He paused after ten steps, eating a doggie treat attached to a rolled up piece of paper.

"Lightning," I called in a raspy voice, "Come here!" I beckoned him back to the closet. "You've got to stay right beside me. Now behave, or else."

Lightning nimbly leaped up the steps to me, then pushed out his front feet as though he was bowing to me. *Nice, at least he knows who's the boss.* However, a big yawn and a stretch told me I was wrong. He laid down the rolled paper and chewed the doggie treat. I stooped down, picked up and unrolled the paper. A concert announcement for this evening. But handwritten in black letters were the words, "**Zanadu boys—Attendance will be hazardous to your health.**" I rerolled the paper and jammed it into my pants pocket. I grabbed Lightning, coiled his leash around my wrist, and worked my way back through the clothes. I poked my head out into the room. No one there. Stepping out firmly, I closed the closet door, and walked to the next room.

Pausing at the doorway, I snuck into the next room, and wandered over to Pete. I breathed a small sigh of relief.

The tour guide had directed everyone's attention toward the front of the room. "This is the throne room," the guide announced.

"You could mistake this room for a church due to its two stories of columned arches, rich gold-covered decorations, and the marble staircase ending on a landing with a place for a throne." Behind the empty space for the throne was an elaborate painting of Jesus Christ surrounded by several paintings of kings and the twelve apostles.

"Before we move to the next room, please remember that we must all stay together." The guide's eyes stopped on me. "All ages will benefit from the information I have for you and I especially wouldn't want our younger guests such as this cute blond-haired boy to become lost."

Mom and Dad captured my attention. Mom's crossed arms and Dad's finger motion demanded I talk to them. I swallowed and walked Lightning over.

"I don't expect my boys to get lost. Do I make myself clear?" Dad placed both hands on my shoulders and tilted his head to the side.

"Yes, sir. I understand." I nodded my head, raising my eyebrows. "I won't get lost."

"Alright. Go back to your friend."

"Hey, that's a neat gadget." I poked Pete in the ribs as we got to the king's dining room. Simultaneously, the thick wooden table at the center of the room lowered as the floor parted beneath it.

The tour guide kept talking in her relaxed British accent. "The servants in the kitchen would set the ornately carved table for the king with all the food he desired (including food for guests when necessary). Then they raised the table laden with the feast through the floor, ensuring the food remained hot. Additional food could be brought up through a food lift on this floor also."

"I'd like that kind of table in my house." Pete kept his voice low. "Then I'd have servants serve me French toast I could eat while wearing my pajamas."

I chuckled at the thought. Although Pete loved his German food, breakfast at our house had convinced him that French toast must have been made in heaven. I waited with Pete as Lightning sniffed the floor where the table had been.

"There's got to be a secret passage to the tunnels." I pulled Pete around the room. "Where are they?" We found a few other novelties, such as vents for talking between floors, and laundry chutes to send dirty clothes down to the ground floor for cleaning, but no hidden pathways out of the room.

As we caught up to the main group, Jenna blocked our way.

"Check this out!" she said in a deep whisper to Alex that I thought everyone could hear. "Past that gorgeous living room and dressing room is the bedroom, and in there is a special surprise." Jenna steered us in that direction.

Pete and I failed to see what she was talking about.

"There's a secret door to the best room of the castle. It's called 'the grotto.'" Jenna said.

"Awesome," Pete said and grabbed my arm to drag me forward.

I picked up Lightning and followed Pete, Alex, Jenna, and Thunder through the next two rooms into the bedroom. They all disappeared through a passageway in the wall. I held back with Lightning to figure out how the exit was hidden when closed. The passageway door was disguised as part of a castle "feast scene" painting on the wall next to the king's bed. The outline of the secret door blended into a painted castle door on the wall beneath King Ludwig's family crest. The tour guide, waiting patiently for the last person of the group, saw my wide eyes and open mouth.

"Amazing, isn't it?" she said. "You can't even notice the doorway when the secret door is shut. Would you like me to open and close it again?"

"Sure, that'd be great." I nodded my head.

The tour guide used a hidden latch behind a hanging picture on the opposite wall to shut and open the exit again. When closed, the outline of the door fit exactly into the wall painting. *Perfect camouflage.* When it opened, I stepped into the grotto.

"What took you so long?" Jenna caught my eye as I walked in the grotto. Before I could answer, she said, "Never mind. I love this room. Look at the artificial stalagmites and stalactites lit up by colored lights and listen to the sound of running creek water. There are also a few artificial waterfalls, a small stream, and extra water sounds coming from hidden speakers." As Jenna turned to go, she paused and said to Pete and me, "You two need to keep up or our parents will get suspicious we're doing something wrong."

"Who are you, our personal tour guide?" I said as we exited the grotto passage in an obscure corner of a hallway. "We're doing just fine on our own." I nudged Pete and scratched Lightning's ear. *Man, she's sure being bossy today.*

"Hey, that's secret passageway number one," Alex whispered to all of us. "And next we should see the Singer's Hall, if they haven't closed it for tonight's performance."

"That would be too bad," Jenna sympathized. "I know your parents haven't planned to go to the concert tonight and that you'd like to go. Maybe I can talk to my parents to get your parents to go."

"Yeah, that would be nice." Alex knit his eyebrows together and turned away.

I pushed ahead of Jenna and Alex. We walked past the conservatory through green-tinted glass doors. I put Lightning back on the ground so I could look at the rooms we passed. My eyes swiveled back and forth, discovering intriguing parts of the ancient corridors and rooms as we passed through the study and walked by a door to the food lift from the kitchen.

Alex said to all of us, "Look at that dumb waiter. That's the second secret passage we could use to get around the castle!"

"Actually," I spoke in a fake British accent, "Lightning saw the first secret passage in the king's chambers, inside the wardrobe. The hidden doorway opens into a staircase that could be used as a getaway. This isn't any mysterious passage. There's no disguise. Probably doesn't even work anymore. Watch this."

With that said, I jumped into the dumb waiter with Lightning, made a face, and disappeared.

Chapter 12

TUNNEL TALK

I fell backward as the door slammed shut and the lift dropped for about two seconds. I couldn't see anything. I held my hands in front of my face, but couldn't tell they were there. I stretched out to find the walls. They felt smooth, like concrete. Starting on one side, I quickly worked my way around the shaft feeling for ropes or buttons. The lift was about four-feet wide and three-feet deep. I couldn't touch anything above me. I rubbed my head, which had a slight bump on the back. I had a pounding headache. Lightning jumped up on my leg. I reached down to reassure him. A couple of his licks on my chin made me feel better.

"We'll get out of here, buddy."

I checked the walls again to see if there were any cracks, ledges, or other irregularities in the wall so I could pull myself up, but the walls were smooth.

Suddenly, light shot in from an opening above me. Jenna's face leaned over me about twelve feet up.

"Having a little problem, Gabe?" She mocked me while swinging her blond hair to one side of her neck. "I think we can help."

Pete pushed Jenna out of the way. "Gabe, Alex is working the pulleys on the side. He got the doors open and he'll get you up here. You okay?"

"Yeah, I guess so."

Two minutes later, Alex had pulled me back up to the right level. "I'm glad they put an emergency brake on this contraption. Made for dummies like you. You were too heavy, which caused the system to lock up. I reset the braking system behind this side panel. Next time, think before you act. You almost snapped the wires for the whole contraption."

"We need to find the secret passage for the tunnel. We have to look in unusual places. And I am not a dummy." I brushed myself off, rubbed the back of my head, and grabbed Lightning's leash.

"You were almost a crash dummy." Alex smiled.

I stepped back. "The people that built this machine knew it could get heavy. That's why they had a safety stop built in."

Jenna smirked. "Next time you may not be so lucky."

"Forget it."

Alex looked at me as we walked back to the tour. "Did you see anything today that might mark the secret passages? You're the only one who saw both of them."

"No, I can't remember anything ... except ...," I paused. "I found a concert flyer and there was a specific warning for us." I indicated Alex and me. "The note said attending the concert tonight would be hazardous to our health." I pulled the note out of my pocket and showed it to everyone.

"This was in the secret passage that Lightning found?" Jenna snatched the note from me.

"That's weird." Alex put his hand on his chin. "No one but staff should have access to that area."

I glanced back at my brother. "Yep. You're right. There's no public access. And we're not even planning on going to the concert." I shrugged. "What a worthless note."

In five minutes we caught up with our tour guide, who took us up the winding staircase in the North Tower to the fourth floor.

"Here we have a lounge and the Singer's Hall, inspired by the *Tannhauser* Opera during King Ludwig II's time." The tour guide's voice flowed around the room. "Paintings depicting the *Tannhauser* story were painted on the walls, in alcoves, and around the windows, and from the windows are beautiful views of our three lakes."

I bumped Alex's arm. "Good news—this place is open for a tour. I thought they closed the Hall to tours if there was going to be a concert."

"Yeah," Alex said. "Maybe ..."

"This evening there will be a concert," our guide announced. "We will close the Singer's Hall at 1230 to prepare." She continued as we walked around the room. After the Singer's Hall, we went downstairs. I jumped two to three steps at a time while Lightning rode on my shoulders.

"Here on the ground floor," the tour guide began, "is the castle kitchen."

As the tour guide kept talking, I walked around with Pete looking for another secret passageway. One wall was about forty paces, with the others even longer. I couldn't smell food of any sort, just a musty rock wall smell. I stood near a counter with glazed pottery, running my hand over the smooth edge. We passed huge cooking bowls sitting on open shelves, and I tapped the bottoms of several pots and pans hanging from the ceilings. King Ludwig II's crest decorated the fireplace.

I tugged on Pete's shirt to get his attention. "Look around the fireplace for loose stones."

We pushed on all the stones we could reach. I ducked my head into the fireplace, touching the grate and looking into the flue. No clues. No tunnel. Thunder and Lightning sniffed wherever I pointed. They sniffed and sneezed because of the dust. I patted their heads. There were two spits for cooking meat, a built-in oven, and other places for cooking and heating. Touching, feeling the cracks, and having the dogs nosing around didn't bring any luck.

"Thunder and Lightning," I said in a low voice. "Sniff over there." I pointed to a separate heating stove made of porcelain decorated with Chinese-looking art sitting alone near the far wall from where we entered the kitchen.

"Pete, did you find a secret passage yet?" I kept my voice low and soft.

"Nothing here, but I know King Ludwig liked to move around without being seen." Pete motioned past the open hearth. "There's a bookcase over there on that wall."

I saw a small crest from King Ludwig painted by the bookshelf. Lightning and Thunder sniffed near the bookcase, scratching at the rock floor. Pete coaxed a book off a shelf, but immediately put the leather-bound volume back when the tour guide caught his eye and shook her head.

"Good try," I whispered to Pete. I yanked on Thunder and Lightning's collars to get them back under direct control. "Where is the tunnel?"

"Gotta be here somewhere. One place the King would have liked to visit is the kitchen—for a snack." Pete shrugged his shoulders, waiting for another place to look.

"I'm sure there have to be more secret passages, letting the King move from floor to floor and room to room without being spotted," Jenna said as she joined Pete and me.

"The castle's foundation was laid in 1869 and the king died in 1886 in the summer." Alex's informative memory started clicking as he joined us. "So even though he didn't finish the castle, he did complete a great deal. If there aren't any more secret passageways we can find, it's probably because he didn't have time to build more of them."

We walked down several more flights of stairs. As we joined our families we took a sloping tunnel exit to leave the castle.

"I thought we were on the bottom floor in the kitchen," I said.

"Counting floors in Germany is different than in America," Pete said. "That's why the first floor of our hotel is actually one level above the street. Anyway, the floors we came down after the kitchen were below the ground if you look at how the hill slopes up to the castle."

"Then a connecting tunnel between the two castles could have been built secretly after they had built a few floors," I said.

"The tunnel is a myth!" Pete said as he stopped, looked me full in the face, and pushed one hand to the side. "You need to forget it. Did we find a tunnel?"

"No," I said. "We didn't. But I'm not giving up. I saw a connecting tunnel on the engineer's map."

As we walked out the tunnel exit of the castle, Dad said to Mom, "Why don't we all go over to Mary's Bridge over the Poellat Gorge. It's not a long walk and there's a superb view of the castle. The walk will give the boys and dogs a little more exercise."

"That's a good idea," Karl Schultz said, "but I had planned on getting the family ready for a little caving this afternoon." He stood in the roadway, half-turned to go.

"Karl, we won't be long. Can you meet us in an hour and a half before you leave?" Dad said. "I know the boys brought their caving gear today. We're just going to take some pictures, do a little shopping, and then we'll meet you in the parking lot."

"Okay, we'll see you in an hour and a half." Karl shook hands with Dad and walked away.

"Dad, can you really see the castle from the Gorge?" I moved toward the trail.

"You bet." He pointed up the hill to the path. "Let's go."

We hiked for ten minutes up a well-maintained trail with rock walls on either side, and through the fall forest over to the Gorge. Once we stood on Mary's Bridge, I saw the lake behind Neuschwanstein. The castle appeared to be suspended on its steep hill held up by the pine tree forest. Roaring water gushed off a cliff below me, pounding the rocky outcrops and thundering into a large pool at least a hundred feet below the bridge. The crystal clear pool created a rushing stream, which wound its way through boulders and forest past Neuschwanstein to the lake. I stood at the green metal girder closest to the castle, which people used as a railing, taking it all in.

I was pretty content—*until I heard the scream.*

Chapter 13

HIDDEN ENTRANCE

The scream pierced the air again. I looked to my right. Mom and Dad were at the far end of the bridge, oblivious to the noise. Alex and Thunder were close, but watching something to my left. I turned to locate the screamer. A dark-skinned lady and her little girl stood out in the crowd since they both wore floppy straw sun hats, large sunglasses, and blue flower-print dresses. They were about thirty feet away on my left, leaning out over the railing and pointing down under the bridge. I ran to the bridge railing and looked down. Lightning, suspended by his leash and harness, swayed out from under the bridge like a pendulum. Every few seconds there was a jerk and the swinging arc lengthened.

I leaned over the bridge railing, shouting, "Lightning, don't move."
Lightning continued to wave his paws and struggle.

With little time to act, I raced toward the women. The dark-skinned girl, about six years old, kept grabbing at Lightning's leash, which was woven through several posts in the railing. Its knotted leather end caught on each post for a second, then released, dropping Lightning another six inches. The girl couldn't stop the

73

leash from slipping through her fingers. I rushed around her left side and slammed my left hand against the last foot of the sliding leash, wedging the dark cowhide against a post. With my right hand, I clamped down on the brown leather knot.

"Need some help?" Alex's relaxed voice made me mad.

"You could say that," I snapped back.

Alex sniggered as he sauntered closer. "Do you want me to take a picture before you pull him back in?"

I kicked out at him after he walked up and stood next to me. "Quit joking around. Help me get Lightning up. I don't think now is the time for pictures."

"He's in no danger now. You've got him." Alex thumped me in the middle of the back, but I didn't lose my grip on the leash. Alex bent down, pulling on the leash to raise Lightning. In five minutes, my little dog was back on the bridge.

I thanked the lady and her daughter. The girl's long black hair swung forward as she knelt down and petted Lightning. He returned the kindness by jumping up and licking her face thoroughly.

The slender lady stepped closer to me. "What happened? How did your dog fall through the bars in the railing?"

My breathing slowed as I ruffled Lightning's long hair. "I must have let go of the leash while looking at the castle. Lightning likes to play a 'weaving game' where he goes in and out of the different bars. He must have lost his balance."

"I'm glad you were able to save him." The girl looked up at me, white teeth flashing in a big grin.

I grabbed Lightning, pressing his orange-blond mane against the side of my face. "He's my best friend. I'd never want to lose him."

After talking for a few minutes, we said goodbye. Holding tightly to Lightning, I gazed over the edge of the bridge again, but Mom and Dad cut our time short.

"Take one last look," Dad said as he walked over to Alex and me. "There's the Alpsee Lake and the Hohenschwangau castle."

We both nodded. As we left the bridge, following twenty feet behind Mom and Dad, Alex grabbed my shirtsleeve and turned me toward a wooden sign. "See? The gorge trail down by the waterfall is short. We could hike to our parking lot."

Without hesitation, I ran to ask permission. "Mom and Dad, can Alex, Thunder, Lightning, and I walk back to the van on the gorge trail?"

Mom slid an arm around Dad's waist and gazed into his eyes with a mischievous grin. "I think that trail's too steep for me in these shoes. A carriage ride back down the hill to the van would be nice. We could also do a little *shopping*." She widened her eyes, smiled, and squeezed Dad's arm.

Dad leaned his head to one side as though he was thinking. He put his arm around Mom's waist before he responded. "Okay, sounds good to me." Looking at Alex and me, he kept talking. "Boys, don't take too long. And keep the dogs out of the water. See you in no later than one hour."

"Alright," we said in unison. At the trailhead, we both stopped and looked at our watches to check the time. Alex set an alarm on his watch for sixty minutes and took off with Thunder, racing in front of Lightning and me to the top of the stairs. I darted after them with Lightning in tow. I jumped down the asphalt and concrete stairway quicker than Alex, charging to the front. The stairs gave way to a flatter path of buried logs and packed dirt. I increased my speed as we neared the waterfall.

"Gabe." Alex's heavy breathing behind me sounded pretty close even after three minutes of leaping stairs and running hard.

"What?" I said, stopping and turning around.

Alex passed me as I paused to see what he wanted. He had tricked me to get in the lead. I wasn't going to let that happen. I caught up to him and passed him in two minutes. Gasping for air from the effort, I stopped again and said, "Hey Alex, let's take the dogs off their leashes and put them on voice control so we can all enjoy this."

Lightning and Thunder precariously balanced on boulders about fifteen feet from the water's edge of the pool created by the first set of waterfalls. Both looked expectantly at Alex, with their ears perked up and their backs straight.

"Not a bad idea." Alex sagged against a tree, catching his breath. "But we have to keep them out of the water."

"That's easy," I said. "The river episode yesterday was an accident. It won't happen again." I felt pretty sure the dogs could handle themselves after the scolding we gave them before dinner last night.

"Well ..." Alex paused. "Okay, I agree."

"Voice control, Lightning. Listen up." Lightning cocked his head to show he was listening.

"Run means okay. Whistle ... return. Water ... no!" I held Lightning's muzzle in my hand and looked into his eyes. For emphasis, on the word 'no' I tapped Lightning on the nose with my finger hard enough to ensure I had his attention. *Don't make me regret this, boy.* I picked him up, gave him a big hug, and set him down. He looked up at me and sat down next to my right leg.

Alex gave the same commands and warnings to Thunder. Then, we packed the dogs' leashes away in our backpacks and watched them take a few free steps. They hesitated and looked back. The smooth path was surrounded by elm, oak, and pine trees growing in rocky, boulder-strewn earth. Cliffs and rock walls greeted us as the trees thinned out near the water. The sun-speckled stones and packed earth made the hike easy. I could feel the warmth reflected by sun-baked rocks that lay in the middle of the gorge. The stream roared at the base of the hundred-foot waterfall, but quieted down a bit further downstream. The air carried the smell of wet earth, damp trees, and lots of water nearby. The clear stream raced down the mountainside, gathering in a few areas to make splashy five-foot runoffs into thirty-foot wide emerald green pools beneath.

"Go on," I said to Lightning. "Run." My face stretched into a smile as Lightning streaked away, racing Thunder down the hill.

"Hey." Alex put his hand on my shoulder.

"What?"

"I was thinking. We saw two secret passages in the castle today, but not the tunnel. If there *is* a tunnel, there's got to be another secret passage," Alex said.

"Duh!" I said. "I thought there might be a specific sign to mark the tunnel or secret passageways, but I didn't see anything. I also want to know how Dad already had paperwork for Thunder and

Lightning to get into the castle. He's never used them before." I stopped talking and looked down the hill. I didn't want to talk now. We were outside. Sun and warmth put a spring in my step. The dogs were running and I wanted to be doing the same thing. "I'm free … eee … eee … eee … eee," I sang out as I threw my arms in the air and bolted down the path, leaving Alex standing still for a few seconds. I looked behind me. Alex sprinted after me, but I was faster.

Down on the stony bank of the creek, I slid to a stop, scattering pebbles in all directions. A flash of light caught my attention. I looked again, but the light had disappeared.

"Come here." I waved Alex over. "I saw the sun bounce off something shiny. It's not there now, but there's some kind of opening across the creek on the other side of the hill!"

Alex leaped over and around three large rocks to reach me. He squinted, shielding his eyes from the sun with his hand, and looked in the direction I pointed.

"I don't see anything."

"You have to be at just the right angle, down at my level." I pointed again.

Alex leaned down closer to my arm, putting his chin on my shoulder. "Yeah, now I see it. It's pretty big. I'm thinking there's a cave."

"Come on, let's see what's inside."

"We can't. Mom and Dad will be waiting for us down at the car because the carriage ride doesn't take that long. Besides, we only have forty minutes left. It will take at least half an hour to get down to the parking lot."

I threw a stone with all my might at the rock face across the water. "You're chicken. Mom said she wanted to shop before we get there. We should be okay. Besides, the hour mark was an 'about' time, not an 'exact' time. If we're a few minutes late, they won't care. Let's go take a quick peek."

"I am not chicken. I'm careful, but I'll go," Alex agreed. "We'll have to be quick and clean."

Chapter 14

TYRANNY OF TIME

Alex's through-the-teeth whistle stopped the downward momentum of the dogs. They both made 180 degree turns and dashed back up the hill to us.

"Whoa, settle down," I told Lightning as he jumped up to my chest, wagging his tail, and creating quite a breeze.

After looking around, we found flat stones sticking out of shallow water that gave us a zigzag pathway to the other side. With hands held out for balance, we teetered, slipped, and jumped to dry ground. No one got wet.

As I got closer to the cave entrance, I looked back across the stream. Big boulders around the opening blocked out the view of most of the other side. When I turned back, Alex and the dogs had started to go inside the three-foot-high and two-foot-wide cave opening. Thunder tried to push ahead first. Lightning didn't like that, so he pushed ahead of Thunder. Both dogs bumped into Alex, who was in front of all of us. He almost fell over since he was leaning forward into the hole.

"Stop! Stop, everybody!" Alex yelled as he pushed us all back. "We can't all go through the opening at once. Besides, it's dark in there and I can't see anything. I need my caving light."

We all backed away from the opening. Dropping our backpacks, Alex and I pulled out spelunking lights that we wore on our heads. We turned them on.

"Gloves." Alex reminded me.

"Right," I muttered. *Stop telling me what to do. This prep is taking too long. We need to get into the cave!* If we had more time, I would have told him off. But he could be stubborn and I didn't want to waste the time on him. I glared at him and slapped my leather gloves together in irritation. I swung my backpack in place, then headed toward the entrance.

Thunder and Lightning paced back and forth, wagging their tails. Waiting.

Alex and I stood face to face at the cave entrance. We checked each other's lights, batteries, gloves, and extra climbing equipment. After two minutes, I pulled away. "This is taking way too much time. Let's go." I studied the cave entrance. "These edges are rough, but I think we can get through without messing up our clothes. We'll have to be careful to stay out of trouble." I looked back at Alex to see if he heard me.

"I'm the one who suggested gloves, remember?" Alex shot back.

I made a gorilla face and grunted at him. *He's always trying to be the boss.* I had to have the last word. I said, "I already knew that."

Not waiting for any more comments, I ducked inside the opening, went forward several feet, and halted. Alex bumped into me with his head. "Watch it," I snarled. "Turn your light on if you can't see." Thunder and Lightning wiggled past me on the left. I switched on my headlamp. The beam cut through particles of dust floating in the air and put the dogs in the spotlight. They sniffed and snorted as dust tickled their noses.

Light from Alex's headlamp revealed the jagged edges of the tunnel on my left. Hunched over, our beams lit up most of the gray rocky interior infused with scattered multi-colored crystals that glowed in the light. After traveling about fifteen feet more, I noticed the tunnel had widened and emptied into a much larger space. The ceiling was higher here.

"Alex, look at this chamber." I said. "Huge."

The chamber was about a hundred feet long, seventy feet wide, and thirty feet high, with stalactites and stalagmites. A fairly straight path about three feet wide swept through the stalagmites, making a half-left turn at about ten paces into the open space.

"Gabe, over here."

I followed Alex as the cavern made a steep descent, far steeper than the place where the water flowed down the gorge. Openings appeared at uneven intervals on each side of the cave. A few were tunnels, but I found one that looked like a room hollowed out of the rock. Since our two headlamps lit only the area in front of us, my sense of direction became confused by the twisting turns and side openings. The tunnel seemed to wind under the gorge. A cool breeze blew up from the lower part of the cavern. The air was a bit moist.

"Look, the tunnel floor is becoming a little flatter and smoother," Alex said after a bit. The tunnel was fifteen feet wide at this point and there were no stalagmites. Powdery dust covered the entire floor and footprints going in both directions filled the area. "Looks like someone made this part flatter to allow for a large walking space."

I looked at my watch. "We'll have to figure it out later. We've been down here fifteen minutes. Time to get back."

Alex looked at his watch to confirm. "Yep. We're going to be late. Let's go."

"Where are the dogs?" I asked. Alex and I swung our headlamps in every direction.

No dogs.

I hadn't been paying attention. *Crazy dogs. We can't waste the time.*

A faint yipping sound came floating up from the lower cave. We walked further into the cave and the sound got stronger.

"Lightning, where are you?" I said. "Keep talking, boy." The sound echoed off the walls.

Lightning responded with more barking.

We broke into a trot and a few minutes later found Thunder and Lightning trying to dig out a small animal. Dust and dirt flew everywhere. Tails wagging, the dogs surrounded a hole, getting low to the ground with their front paws, alternately sticking their snouts into the hole to bite or grab and using their forepaws to dig out the animal. When their noses were in the hole, the trapped animal kicked out dirt and dust, choking the dogs. They danced back and forth like a tag team.

I walked over to Lightning and pulled him back from the hole. "Lightning, no more. We're leaving."

Lightning's dust-covered snout was like a mask. He cocked his head, looking at me with large, wistful eyes and pulling back to the hole.

"No. I *said* we're leaving." I picked Lightning up, threw him over my shoulder on top of my backpack, and started walking back up the slope to the entrance of the cave.

"Come on, Thunder." I heard Alex order his dog. "Time to go."

We jogged back to the entrance of the cave. *We're gonna be late!* I almost kicked myself. *That could mean another strike against us.*

Outside the cave, Alex and I brushed the dust off each other, our backpacks, shirts, hair, and the dogs. *Thankfully, we've stayed alert and kept our clothes from getting too rumpled or dirty.*

Alex said, "If we hurry, we might make it. Look at the time. Let's mark this place and then go. We've got to run to get back!"

"We don't have time," I stomped my foot, clipping my words short. "We won't be back this way again anyway."

Alex ignored me, took out his black-light paint spray can, and quickly painted a line in the corner made by the cliff and the cave entrance.

Alex looked at the dogs. "Okay, boys, we need to make up some time," he said. "Down the hill. Run!"

Thunder and Lightning took off without another command. They crossed the stream, weaving back and forth around the jumbled rocks. Lightning ran circles around Thunder as they both jumped over and leaped from rock to rock. *They're getting too far ahead.* I whistled through my teeth; then bellowed, "Thunder, Lightning, *STOP!*"

Both dogs made a tight circle, running back toward us.

Alex and I hustled down the hill, bouncing from one rock to the next. The dogs met us, turned around, took off first, followed by me, then Alex. Halfway down the hill, Alex's body lunged past me without warning, flying into space toward a green pool ten feet below the rocky edge we skirted. He blurred past me before I could react. Too late. Nothing could prevent his face-first descent. As I watched from the small cliff's edge, my mind took a split-second picture of the scene. Alex's flailing arms, wide-open mouth and eyes, and legs stretched out behind him while suspended in mid-air clashed with the peaceful scenery. The calm blue sky, unmoving stony riverbanks and quiet rainbow-colored pine, elm, and birch trees behind him gave no hint of the crazy, out-of-control disaster in progress. I laughed inside.

Breaking the peaceful atmosphere, Alex yelled an extended, "Whoa!"

Thunder and Lightning, about fifteen feet in front of me, heard Alex cry out. They stopped, then dashed back to see Alex smash into the water.

When he popped back up in about four feet of water, I clapped my hands and laughed. "Good job, Alex. When did you decide to take flying lessons? Did you have a good landing?"

Alex yelled, "Get off my back. This is a disaster."

He spluttered, slapped the water in anger, and threw a small stick in my direction. It missed me by ten feet.

"Why did we have to go look at that cave," Alex complained as he stood up in shallower water, dripping wet. He looked at me. "It's your fault."

"No way. We were making good time. You're the one that wanted to go swimming."

"I tripped over a rock because I was rushing to avoid being late. If we hadn't looked at the cave, we would've had plenty of time."

"Yeah. And that's my fault?" I put my hands on my hips and shrugged my shoulders. "Why don't you take the blame? I didn't trip you."

He tried to splash me with water, but I backed up in time. Then, he studied the creek bed for a moment. "Hey, this looks like a natural water slide. I bet I can slide down the rocks to the parking lot faster than running around boulders. Since I'm wet anyway, I might as well have a little fun if I'm going to be in trouble." With his waterproof backpack on his chest, Alex began sliding down the creek in areas where it was smooth and sloshing through parts of the stream that were more level.

Thunder and Lightning's ears leaned forward as they darted back and forth toward the water, wherever Alex slid down a chute or stood up. Up and down the rocky bank they darted, ending up at a green pool with a five-foot drop. Alex washed over the waterfall with a big splash. Growling, Thunder crouched down on his forelegs as he started to make a plunge, hesitated, then bunched his muscles up, preparing to spring into the pool again. Lightning stood right next to him, yipping and bouncing like a fluffy ball.

"Don't," I called out to them. "Remember the voice commands. You're supposed to stay out of the ..."

Thunder, followed by Lightning, flew through the air and into the pool of water. The dogs let out howls of delight while dog-paddling to a shallow area.

"... water." I finished and kicked some rocks in frustration. "Doesn't anyone remember we're not supposed to get wet?" I walked to edge of the pool to drag Lightning out of the water.

"Gabe," Alex groaned through clenched teeth. "I wrenched my back on that last drop. The bank is steep here. Give me a hand so I can get out and begin to dry off."

Alex paddled with only his right hand to shallow water. His face was wrinkled at the forehead, his jaw clenched, and he got on one knee in the shallow area, close to the edge. Reaching his hand for mine, he winced in pain.

I reached out to help him and felt myself losing balance. I fell forward as he stood up and leaned back, pulling me into the water.

Fooled again. Standing up, I ripped off my waterproof backpack and jumped onto Alex's back to dunk him in the water. We wrestled for a minute until I swung my left leg around both of his and he went under. *How could I ever trust him?*

He broke water and dunked me. The dogs began chasing each other, when Alex's watch alarm sounded. Our hour was gone.

"Come on," I said. "Going down by the stream will be faster than getting back over to that winding walking path." I went first as we slid down the rocks, water chutes, and mini-water falls, rapidly nearing the trail to the parking lot. We had a blast. The rocks were smooth and the water cushioned our falls. Our clothes got wet and dirty, but there were no rips or tears. *Being wet will be bad enough,* I reminded myself.

Alex and I sloshed out of the water where the trail turned back toward the parking lot and called the dogs over. With tails waggin' and body's wigglin', Lightning and Thunder stood next to us to shake off the water, spraying us all over. We held up our hands in protest, but they kept on shaking. We looked like a muddled mess!

"Gabe," Alex said with a grin as we started running down the path, "I don't think we stand a chance."

"Yep." I nodded. "We are headed for big T-R-O-U-B-L-E!"

Chapter 15

STRIKE TWO

As we broke out of the trees, the noise of confusion caught my attention.

Tourists strolling in the village road scattered as a pure white draft horse harnessed to a red and green carriage bolted through the scrambling people, veering left, right, and then racing down the incline.

I ran onto the street for a clearer view, shoving Alex out of my way. "A runaway horse! Up the street."

"There's no driver. Get back!" Alex jerked me back onto the sidewalk.

I wrestled my arm out of his grasp and shoved him in the shoulder, then turned back to the action by standing on the edge of the sidewalk.

Between the runaway and us, people buying treasures to take home had crowded the street, shops, and gift stores. The clattering of horseshoes hitting the pavement and angry shouts ruined the village's quiet. The street emptied quickly.

A mother dressed in black pants and a pink blouse cried out, "Wolfgang! Wolfgang!" as she searched for her boy in the jammed sidewalk area. Her hand cupped around her mouth, she shouted and looked in every direction. She was up the hill from us, about four buildings away. The runaway horse was even further up the hill behind her, pounding down the steep grade.

The neighing horse's head shook back and forth as it tried to shake the carriage off its back. Nostrils flared, the horse ran the carriage into the wooden posts of a covered sidewalk in front of a store. The crash echoed and a floorboard in the carriage flew up into the air. Alex and I snagged Thunder and Lightning by their collars and knelt next to a blue Mercedes parked on the street to watch.

Up the hill, not too far from us, a small boy, about five years of age, ran into the middle of the street where he began to play with a small red top—spinning the toy and watching it dance around the pavement, spin erratically, then stand in one place before toppling over. Mom and Dad stood on a sidewalk on the opposite side from the youngster. The boy seemed unaware of the racket of the horse and carriage and the people screaming as they fled the street. He picked up the top, wound the string tightly, and prepared to spin the gadget again.

His mother saw him. She struggled against the crowd, screaming, "Wolfgang, Wolfgang, get off the street." She waved a white handkerchief frantically, but since she was still three buildings away, rescuing her boy was impossible.

The racing horse darted to the left and collided with a restaurant. The wooden and metal carriage slammed into the corner of the building. People scattered, splinters of wood flew, and grinding noises came from the metal and concrete. The carriage righted itself as the horse's pumping legs pulled the wreck back into the street, heading right toward Wolfgang.

"Lightning, sic 'em," I yelled, releasing him and letting him dash into the street towards the unsuspecting boy. Lightning's reddish-blond hair streamed behind him as he ran. Thunder followed, a close second. I was next and Alex was two steps behind.

"Run, Wolfgang!" I screamed, but my voice couldn't penetrate the screams and shouts coming from all around the boy.

The distance between the horse and boy was closing. The dogs, Alex, and I were at least thirty feet away. The boy looked up and smiled at me.

"Get out of the street," I shouted without breaking stride. My pointing finger must have meant something because the boy moved from his crouched position and looked to his left, then turned around to see the rampaging horse and carriage. He froze with legs spread wide, his arms by his side. The top tumbled out of his hand.

In seconds the horse would crush the boy. Thunder and Lightning, barking continuously, had closed the distance between them and the boy to ten feet. I was right on their tails. Alex was several steps behind me.

Thunder and Lightning reached the boy first and slipped past him at incredible speed. The horse's white mane flared to the left as the animal slammed to a stop five feet from Wolfgang. It reared on its back legs, kicking the air with its front hooves and banging them into the asphalt street near the dogs. The dogs ran back and forth, barking and dancing away from the slashing feet. The angry beast neighed and snorted, prancing closer to the boy. Its front legs lifted in the air again and descended directly at the petrified lad.

I had reached the boy. I threw my arms around Wolfgang, drawing his head into my chest as I rolled hard right next to Thunder's darting form. I closed my eyes tightly and pulled up my legs to keep Wolfgang in place. I rolled and rolled away from those slashing hooves. No sharp hooves cut into my flesh, but on my first roll, I heard them pounding into the asphalt near my head. I peeked with one eye.

Alex stood in front of the horse with Thunder and Lightning on either side.

"Settle down," Alex said with both arms raised, palms facing the horse.

The white animal flicked its eyes left and right to locate the dogs. Its flared nostrils snorted. Still struggling against the harness, the horse arched its neck and shook it left and right.

Alex caught the reins on the third try.

"Heel," he called to Thunder and Lightning. Both dogs moved in front of the horse. They sat down and waited. Alex placed his hand above the horse's nose, between the leather harnesses that held the bit in place. Lowering his volume, Alex calmed the horse with soothing words and steady motions.

I picked myself and Wolfgang up off the ground, stood him up, and brushed him off. A few people ventured back into the street.

"Pferd!" the boy yelled as he pointed to the mare that stood shaking its mane.

"That's right, Wolfgang," I said, "It's a horse." I looked at the brown-haired, brown-eyed boy. He was dressed in dark green lederhosen, brown shoes, white socks, and a white shirt.

Just then Wolfgang's mother rushed up and pulled the boy out of my grasp. She hugged him, squeezing tightly while swaying left to right. She released him for a second, kissed him on the cheek, and then hugged him again. Her face was damp with tears as she finally set Wolfgang on the ground, bent down to his level, and let loose with a string of German words I couldn't understand. She finally looked my way, walked over with Wolfgang, and made him say, "Thank you."

I nodded and said, "You're welcome." Wolfgang and I shook hands and they walked away. My attention turned to Alex.

A short German man, dressed in lederhosen, a white shirt, and a green German hat with pheasant feathers talked with Alex. As I walked up, the plump man expressed his thanks. He took the reins and trudged up the hill, leading the horse that pulled the almost demolished carriage.

Mom and Dad hadn't moved from where we first saw them. They motioned for us to come over. Packages and bags lay around their feet.

Dad said, "Amazing rescue. Job well done."

"That poor woman was hysterical," Mom said. "I'm proud of how you handled that whole situation. You're brave young men."

Dad glanced at his watch. "And you're late. What have you ...?" Dad paused and took a good look at our wet and dirty condition. His voice got louder. "What have you been doing?"

"We had a small accident," I said, picking up Lightning and stroking him, even though dirt from the stream had matted his hair into knots.

Mom shook her head. She closed her eyes, breathed deeply, then surveyed us with dismay. "Boys! What did you do? Your hair is a mess and your clothes are soaking wet. I'd like an explanation." Her voice had gone up in pitch. She stiffened her back, clasped her hands in front, raised her eyebrows, and set her lips in a tight line.

I said, "Well, we went down the path in the gorge, but Alex fell into the water. The dogs jumped in after Alex. I went in later. Now we're all wet." I attempted to look sorry. I tilted my head forward, looked at the ground, and shuffled my feet to show I was not a happy camper.

"We can't do anything else until you're changed and dry again!" She hustled us off to the van. "Okay, boys, get some dry clothes and a towel out of the extra camping gear we brought, and go to that outhouse over there and change clothes." She pointed to a small building with restroom signs about fifty yards away.

We took some clothes out of the extra camping supplies in the van and stuffed them in a carry bag, making sure the other spare clothes didn't get messed up. We went to the restroom, dried off, changed, and then I combed my hair. Now I felt much better. I looked at my wet clothes. *No worse for the wear due to our little adventure.* Outside the restrooms, we both used our damp towels to dry Thunder and Lightning as best we could. After cleaning up, we went back to the parking lot. Dad was by himself, sitting in the rear of the van with the rear hatch up, eating a soft pretzel and drinking water.

"Out with it boys. Why did you have an accident?" Dad said through bites of pretzel and gulps of water.

I started. "Dad, we saw this little hole in the side of the gorge that looked interesting, and ..."

Alex interrupted, "We looked inside a little bit. The hole looked really small, but after we got inside ... well, there was a huge cave!"

"The tunnel in the cave headed right toward Neuschwanstein castle," I said. "I know that's where it goes."

"Boys, boys," Dad stopped us. "Regardless of what you saw, cave or no cave, and where you thought the tunnel went, you didn't meet us at the agreed time. You know what that means." He sighed and shook his head.

Alex and I looked at each other. *Yeah, we know.* My shoulders slumped a little and I plopped down on one of the rocks bordering the parking lot.

I bet that cave confirms my earlier idea about a tunnel exit from Neuschwanstein castle. But now that we're in trouble, there is probably NO WAY Alex and I will be allowed to go back and explore more. I bet we'll be grounded. Why couldn't Alex have been more careful! I sneaked a quick look at him and my jaw tightened up. *It was your fault,* I accused him silently. *We still would have been late, but the consequences would have been less.* I leaned over, running my hands through my crazy blond hair.

Mom arrived, working next to Dad to put a few items in the rear of the van. I tried to catch her eyes to get a little sympathy by looking sad. She didn't look at me.

"Because you both risked yourselves to rescue that little boy, your discipline for being late and getting in the water won't be as bad." Dad said. "However, you're now at Strike Two. That means the rest of the day you're going to spend all your time with your mother and me, doing whatever we do. No friends, no caving ..."

I knew it. My favorite thing to do—gone.

"I've already spoken to the Schultz family," Dad finished.

For a second, I felt defeated. My shoulders slumped lower and I glared at Alex again for his clumsiness. He glared right back at me.

Alex probably thinks we were late because I went too far into the cave. He's the problem, not me.

"Strike Three and you'll be out!" Dad got out of the back of the van, closed the hatch, and went to the front of the car to talk with Mom.

Strike Three would be a bummer. Grounding for a month with no electronic games, TV, friends, or after-school activities. I crouched down next to Lightning and said, "Don't worry, little buddy. But no more playing in the water for you." Without thinking, I rubbed his head hard and almost knocked him over.

Alex, who was standing between Lightning and Thunder, grabbed his dog around the neck and gave him a big hug.

We left the van and walked up to the entryway located inside the courtyard of Hohenschwangau castle. "Now that we're together this afternoon, we are going to take another castle tour," Mom lectured, assuming her normal home-school teacher role. We walked directly from the parking lot up a series of gray steps made of concrete in some parts and cobblestones in another. The path switched back and forth three times before reaching a long, winding cobblestone pathway that led past a small chapel through a wooded area to the castle itself. A small wall surrounded the castle's main and secondary building. We went under an arch in the courtyard wall and into the waiting area. In the center above the arch were two shields, one with the Bavarian crest, and one with the Hohenschwangau crest.

Hohenschwangau, which was much smaller than Neuschwanstein, sat on a hill easily reached from the city streets in ten minutes. The outside was covered in golden stucco and topped with deep red tiles. The main building had two stories for the king and queen, though other parts of the castle were taller and had more floors. There was an annex for the children to live in, servant's quarters, a separate chapel, and a beautiful garden area with fountains. A visitor could still see two lakes from the courtyard area. The Alpine garden of various flowers from the area captured my eyes with brilliant fall colors.

I fidgeted as we waited to go in, looking for another guard that might not let the dogs in the castle. Then, Dad told us to stay put for a minute. He went across the courtyard and started talking to someone who looked as if he worked at the gate, but he wasn't a guard. The man smiled and nodded his head.

Dad announced when he returned, "Before we go in, take the dogs for a quick walk to make sure they don't have an accident in the castle."

Alex and I walked back down the hill towards the chapel and into the woods. We were back in the courtyard with the dogs five minutes later.

The entryway into the castle was through two heavy wooden doors about eight feet tall. The tour guide led us up a short, wide marble staircase, past white and light blue walls to the first level. The guide was a woman about five-and-a-half-feet tall, slim, and able to easily move from one place to the next, pointing out the best features while telling the history of the castle. When the guide moved us from room to room, Mom gave her home-school version of Hohenschwangau's background that wasn't covered by the lady tour guide's remarks.

"King Ludwig II spent time here as a boy and during the building of Neuschwanstein," Mom said while we walked up to the first floor entry room. "Neuschwanstein is on a taller hill than Hohenschwangau, and that allowed King Ludwig II to watch the scaffolding and construction of his new home. Hohenschwangau was a medieval knight's castle built in the twelfth century. Crown Prince Maximillian, Ludwig's father, bought the castle ruins in the 1830s and later, when he became king, he reconstructed the castle, completing it in 1855. Hohenschwangau became the family's summer residence and hunting lodge. King Maximillian II lived on the second floor in the main building and his wife, Queen Marie, lived on the first floor. Ludwig and his brother lived in the separate annex we saw before we came in."

I listened to Mom's voice in the background. On the first floor, Hohenschwangau's decorations and gifts to the king appeared delicate and expensive. I kept Lightning away from them. Three gifts were displayed on a table in the second room and looked like miniature fountains made of gold. Another gift on a table in the fourth room was made of expensive china, gilded with gold and hand-painted with country scenes. I was glad Thunder and Lightning's romping in the gorge and sliding down the waterway had exhausted them. Both dogs were quiet and stayed next to Alex and me for the whole tour.

"I haven't seen any secret passage to connect these two castles by a tunnel like the one we saw in the gorge," Alex whispered to me as we climbed stairs to the next level.

I tilted my head a little and cracked a smile. "Must be one here somewhere."

On the second floor, the tour guide stopped by King Maximillian's bedroom. In her British accent, she said, "One mystery that intrigues most visitors is that there is a hidden passageway in this castle."

I knew it. I put my hands on my hips and stuck out my chest as Alex watched. *Now we'll hear about the connecting tunnel between Neuschwanstein and Hohenschwangau.*

The blond-haired guide's hazel-colored eyes looked right at me as she stopped and widened her smile. "King Maximillian had a special passageway built to the Queen's bedroom on the first floor. Even though they slept apart, they could visit each other secretly during the night." She turned and continued to the next room. "Also on the second floor is King Ludwig's observation room, used to follow the building progress of the Neuschwanstein castle through a telescope." As the tour guide continued, my mind went in another direction.

She didn't say anything about a secret passageway between the two castles. There's got to be one. Why else would there be an engineer map? But maybe the map was an idea, not a fact. The tunnel outline was drawn in dashed lines. I didn't know what to think. No mention of an underground connecting tunnel dashed my hopes of an adventurous expedition underground.

The castle tour was about twenty-five minutes long. After the tour, we headed for some shopping at the Marktplatz, the main town shopping area below the Hohenschwangau castle.

"Honey, I'd like to find a German Dirndl dress to wear in the evening to a social function." Mom leaned into Dad's side, hugging his arm.

"Okay." Dad glanced sideways. I could see him eyeing the German shirts and lederhosen worn by many men who lived in the Alps.

"Those lederhosen would look good on you," he looked at Alex and me.

I'm certainly not interested in getting those for me. I groaned a little inside. Mom and Dad always bought us native clothes of the country where we lived. *What's wrong with blue jeans?*

Dad kept talking. "This will look great tonight and match your mother's outfit." Dad bought a pair of lederhosen and a German shirt for each of us.

After the shopping spree, we all went to a fast food wagon called a Schnell Imbiss to get some pommes frites and bratwurst with brotchen. I liked brotchen. Shaped like a hamburger bun with a hard outside, the soft inside was delicious. I bit into the spicy bratwurst wrapped in brotchen that I topped with mustard. I saved the German fries for later. Alex appeared to enjoy his food too. He actually started to smile. *I guess he's done with the sour grapes attitude he had earlier. At least we aren't being punished a lot for our water escapade; although ...* I gave an inward sigh ... *we could have been caving right now with Pete and Jenna.*

Thunder pulled on one of Alex's pant legs, then made sniffing noises near Alex's food.

"Sorry, boy," Alex apologized to Thunder as he took off his backpack, pulled the dog's food out along with a few paper bowls and an old Army canteen. I followed suit with Lightning, unzipping a pocket on my backpack and pulling out some spare camping stuff. Soon, Thunder and Lightning were lapping water from a saucer and enjoying their snack. Afterwards, Alex walked both dogs over to an awning to keep them in the shade and tied their leashes to a pole. He got back to the bench in time to hear Mom's announcement.

"Surprise!" Mom said with wide eyes and a faint smile. "Guess what, boys?"

"What?" I asked. Alex seemed distracted. He kept looking around, checking out the scenery.

"We've got some tickets," Mom said.

"Tickets?" Alex's voice rang out. I think Mom got his attention. He faced her to find out what was happening.

"Do you remember who one of Ludwig's friends was? A composer by the name of Wagner?" Dad said.

"Wagner?" Alex repeated with an excited look. He loved classical music. "I remember. He wrote some amazing music. When's the performance?" Alex stopped breathing, waiting for an answer.

"Tonight," Mom said. "And you'll have to sit with us at the concert."

"Awesome!" Alex slapped his hand on his thigh. "And the concert will be in the castle's Singer's Hall, right?" Alex got up from where he sat, paced a few steps, looked around, then sat back down and said in a more controlled voice, "It will be fun."

"Should be," Dad agreed. "The Schultz family will join us at the Hall."

"There's only one problem," I said. "I found a flyer in Neuschwanstein castle warning Alex and me not to go to the concert or we might get hurt."

"Where is it?" Mom said.

"I threw it away because the flyer got completely soaked when we were coming down the gorge. I couldn't read the warning anymore. It was useless."

"Interesting," Dad replied. "Who else saw the threat?"

"I did," Alex said. "And Jenna and Peter."

"Well, we're not going to let this spoil our time out. I'll make sure someone checks on our rooms at the hotel while we are gone tonight. Since you'll be with us the entire evening, you shouldn't be in any danger."

Man, I've got to sit through a two-hour concert. I crossed my arms, thinking about the dreary music. *Talk about major boredom. I'll have to think of something to do.*

Alex's cheery face didn't make me feel any better.

I'll have to figure a way to make this fun, I vowed to myself. My mind wandered to something else. *Since we began this trip, there have been a lot of weird little things that don't seem right. And it's not our rooms that need to be guarded; Alex and I need protection.* I tapped my chin. Deep down inside, a small voice kept telling me to stay alert.

Chapter 16

THE SINGER'S HALL

We returned to the Alpenblick, had dinner, and went to change into our German outfits for the concert. Before we entered our rooms to change, I tried to convince Mom to let me wear jeans, not lederhosen.

"Mom, the weather's a bit cool to wear lederhosen," I said. "Leather shorts with suspenders may look German, but can't we dress in something warmer?"

"Take your jackets and make sure each of you packs warmer pants in your backpacks," Mom said. "You can change later if you get too cold. We'll be inside most of the time." She followed Dad through their door and didn't wait for an answer.

Shut out, I walked into our room and found Alex studying several yellow pieces of paper. "What's that?" I said.

"A hand-written note. It was lying on the floor when I walked in. Thunder and Lightning must have thought it was trash. They snatched it up and tore it apart."

"Let me see." I grabbed the pieces out of his hands, knelt by my bed, and started spreading them out. Alex crouched next to me.

"There are missing parts," I said.

"The dogs may have eaten some."

Both dogs pushed next to me. Thunder tried to grab a corner scrap. "Stop," I pushed Thunder away. "Alex, tell him to lay down."

Alex and I played with the pieces of paper for a few minutes. The result was a little confusing since we were missing words and letters. I wrote what we could put together on a hotel notepad.

Deep beneath the ground you'll be
If information w … n't see
… watching day and night
Deliver … p … kage by tonight.

A tingle ran up and down my spine. The deadline for delivery was tonight.

Dad's knocking on the door interrupted my thoughts. "Boys, are you ready? Time to leave."

"Almost ready," Alex said. "We'll be right out."

"Hey, Alex," I whispered, "let's not tell Mom and Dad about this. They'll only get more upset and we won't get to go to the concert. We can tell Jenna and Pete and try to solve this on our own. Let's leave our caving gear in our packs with our extra clothes."

Alex looked at me, shrugged his shoulders, and repacked his caving gear into his backpack.

When we walked out the door, we saw Mom wearing a dirndl dress with a shawl. The dress was made of a blue and white gingham fabric and Mom had added a black leather vest with leather lacing. Her blouse was white. Dad had on a German shirt matching our lederhosen. His shirt was black to match her vest. He wore nice black pants and comfortable walking shoes. Our lederhosen were made out of black leather. I wore a dark green shirt and Alex wore a dark blue shirt.

"We look like a regular German family. A tourist family—that is!" Alex joked as we walked to the Go-Mobile.

When we arrived in the Neuschwanstein parking lot, Mom turned around in her seat, smiled, and said, "Thunder and Lightning, you're staying in the van tonight to guard our things."

Our house-on-wheels still contained several bags of food, some climbing gear, tent equipment, cots, extra clothes, and other camping gear. She opened her window a crack to ensure that the dogs would have fresh air.

"Awww, Mom, can't we bring the dogs?" Alex said.

I gave him a sharp look, tilting and slightly moving my head back and forth. I didn't want him to tell Mom why we wanted protection with us.

"No," Mom said as she stepped out of the van.

Dad added, "We talked about this earlier. Strike Two means you stay with us. We don't want Thunder and Lightning with us in the concert. We want our family and others to enjoy this evening's event."

"But Dad, the dogs will behave themselves. And we got them into Neuschwanstein earlier today." Alex petted Thunder.

"And you said we needed the dogs to track down those criminals, right?" I said.

"I've told you what's going to happen. No more arguments."

"Okay," Alex said.

I sighed. I didn't like leaving Lightning behind, but now I wished we hadn't stayed so long in the Poellat Gorge cave. Maybe Alex wouldn't have tripped and fallen into the water and we would have had time to explore it more later.

Alex got out of the Go-Mobile and I followed. As the dogs tried to jump out, Alex and I pushed them back in.

"Stay," I said to Lightning. I crawled back into the van and put him on top of a headrest. He looked like the hair on someone's head. "Lightning, you have a mission now. Guard our stuff." I rubbed his head and smiled. "Be good. Keep the van and our gear safe."

After I backed out, Alex patted Thunder's back. "Stay alert. We'll see you after the show."

Thunder crawled into the back part of the van and lay on top of the pile of gear. His black coat blended in with the black boxes. When I looked from outside the van, I could see the whites of Thunder's eyes staring back at me.

"He's not happy," Alex said as we started walking away. "His ears were down and he put his muzzle flat on the box."

"I think Lightning's okay," I said. I turned to take one last look.

Lightning was leaping lightly from one headrest to another. First to the left armrest to look out the window, next to the seat in front, over to the other armrest and window, and finally back to the passenger seats in the back. "Lightning's making the rounds in the Go-Mobile. No one will bother our stuff."

As we got closer to the center of town, Alex asked Mom, "Can we walk up the hill?"

"No, Dad has arranged for us all to ride by carriage." Mom said.

"After that horse ran away with the carriage before lunch?" I asked.

"I found out that a snake scared that horse," Dad said. "We shouldn't have a problem tonight."

Mom and Dad sat in the back seat of the carriage. As the fancy ride moved up the sparsely lit roadway, Alex and I sat quietly for a few minutes. I looked at the glowing lamps on top of black ornamented posts. The yellow light cast shadows as people walked up the hill. The friendly forest background was lit by smaller lights near the various trails. The gray stone wall next to the asphalt road magnified the sound of the horses' hooves as they echoed in the crisp air. The coach moved slowly through the crowded street, allowing us time to soak in the atmosphere.

We reached the castle about half an hour before performance time. Without the dogs, we easily went through the castle gate and up to the fourth floor to the Lounge area by the Singer's Hall. Mom and Dad immediately moved inside to get the best seats possible—about halfway toward the front. Folding chairs had been placed in rows with a dividing aisle down the middle and larger aisles on either side.

I spotted Pete's stocky build and black hair three rows in front of us. "Pete," I said, calling out his name in a stage whisper. He waved back and said something to his dad. Ten seconds later he sat by me. Out of the corner of my eye, I saw Alex talking with Jenna. Mom and Dad moved up three rows to sit next to the Schultzes and talk.

"Pete," I said, "we found a cave today in the Poellat Gorge. The place was huge! We—"

"Yeah, but we saw a super large cave today!" Pete chimed in. "It must have gone back into the mountain about seventy-five feet and was almost as tall as you."

"Well, that's not as big as the cave we were in." I leaned forward. "And we found a note."

Mom had left her seat and made her way back to me. She placed a hand on my shoulder just as I was about to spill my guts about our great adventure.

"Gabe, you boys will have to be quiet now. The symphony is about to start. No more talking."

Man! Man, oh man! I slammed my back hard into the chair, looked up at Mom with a tight jaw and set lips, then crossed my arms with a big shrug. Now I had to wait. But I was careful. I knew one wrong move and I might be sitting on the other side of all the parents, away from Pete. It would ruin the entire evening. *I'll have to find a way to talk with Pete after the symphony.* I stewed inside.

After a few minutes I cooled down. I hardly paid attention as the first violin played the final tuning pitch for the orchestra. After each set of instruments tuned to that single note, different melodies and notes from violins, flutes, horns, and other strings created a seething sea of sound that slowly faded away. The lights dimmed. The orchestral players all stood and the conductor took his place. The audience applauded as he turned and bowed.

Bored, I decided to play the Sherlock Holmes game, looking for as much detail as possible in everything around me. The most obvious detail was up front. The conductor wore an 1800s costume: a black tuxedo with long tails, a shirt with ruffles and a high collar. The lights dimmed again, meaning the concert was about to begin. Surrounding me, the setting of the old hall with its low lights, rich tapestries, wall hangings, and colorful paintings of country scenes seemed to take me back in time. At the front of the hall, the brightly-lit orchestra's instruments looked like antiques. Musicians, also dressed in 1800s garb, played older-looking string, brass, reed, and percussion instruments. They even had a harpsichord and harp. I felt as if I was listening to an 1885 concert, similar to one that King Ludwig II would have heard. *I guess this isn't as boring as a normal concert.*

The music was soft at first, but swelled to fill Singer's Hall and my ears. Moving inch by inch, I leaned over to talk with Pete. Alex's hand reached over and tapped me on the knee as a warning to stop. I stuck out my tongue at him, then sat back to listen. Thanks to Alex's constant playing of classical music at home, I did recognize a few pieces, such as Handel's "Hornpipe" from his *Water Music* composition and Bach's "Brandenburg Concerto No. Two." Towards the end of the concert, the conductor transformed the softer music into the loud, pounding sounds of the tympani, the blaring of horns, and crescendo of all the strings playing together. I imagined natural thunder and lightning beating outside on the castle roof and windows. As Richard Wagner's masterpiece, "The Ride of the Valkyries," furiously exploded on the stage, Alex and I pounded the beat on our legs. Afterwards, the audience applauded with a standing ovation for this final closing piece.

"Nine o'clock. We need to go back to our gasthaus," Dad said after moving back to our seats.

"Can we walk with the Schultzes while you ride down the hill?" Alex asked.

Mom and Dad looked at each other for a second, then Dad nodded, "Okay, but you have to meet us at the bottom in the parking lot. You can't leave the road and all four of you must walk together. I don't want anything strange to happen. Can I trust you to get it right tonight?"

"Yes," Alex said as I nodded my head.

Pete and Jenna looked at Alex and me with raised eyebrows.

"We'll tell you on the way down the hill," I said, winking.

"Alright, we'll see all of you at the bottom," Mom waved at us from her seat.

As we walked down the stairs, out the gate, and down the hill, I took turns with Alex explaining what we had done and seen at the Poellat Gorge.

"The bad thing is," I said, "that we're supposed to leave tomorrow and go to the Salt Mines and Berchtesgaden."

"Really?" Jenna's eyes got a little brighter in the dim outdoor lights. "We're doing the same thing."

"Super." Alex smiled.

"Yeah," I said. "I bet our parents arranged some more time together in Bavaria. Still …" I paused.

"What?" Pete pushed me in the back.

"There's something strange here. Dad says that all of the people he talked to don't know anything about a cave in the Gorge, especially a cave as large as we saw. The cave legend Dad knows about is from an old book, but no one believes the story anymore. The engineer's map I had doesn't prove anything either."

"How could that be?" Pete kept pushing me down the hill.

"I don't know." I turned around and pushed back at Pete. "Something doesn't make sense. Right before we left for the concert, we found a strange note that the dogs tore up. Here, read what I could make out." I pulled out my hotel notepaper and showed it to Pete at the bottom of the hill, out of the way of the carriages and people strolling in the town.

Deep beneath the ground you'll be
If information w … n't see
… watching day and night
Deliver … p … kage by tonight.

"Mmm," Jenna said. "Let me see that." She pushed her way between Pete and me.

"Looks like someone wants to see some information," she said.

"Yeah. And they're watching you day and night." Pete pointed to the third line.

"That word could be package," Alex joined in.

"Does this mean they'll kill you if they don't get the information by tonight?" Jenna said.

"Kill us?" my head snapped up to look her in the eyes.

She laughed. "I'm only kidding. Besides, what information do you have that they want?"

"I don't know," Alex said. "We don't know anything."

I folded the paper and slid it back into my pocket. I continued to walk with Pete through the town to the parking lot.

"Pete, this is weird," I said. "I've already told you about some of the unusual things that have happened to us on this vacation. And now someone wants information or we'll be killed. Something doesn't add up."

"Don't go any further, guys," Alex called out. "Mom and Dad are only a minute away." He motioned for Pete and me to come back to where the carriage drivers dropped off their riders.

We walked back to Jenna and Alex standing in the dim light and misty evening air.

"Eerie, isn't it?" I said.

"Not really." Pete patted my back. "This is a normal village night. It's not like the city we live in."

The people passing by had put on jackets, shawls, and sweaters. Shop owners were pulling shades over the doors and closing shutters. Outdoor cafes still had people talking and eating while golden light poured out of restaurant windows as they catered to their last guests.

The carriage with Mom and Dad pulled up.

Once on the ground, Dad patted Karl on the back and pointed to the right. "We're parked on that side of the parking lot."

"We're on the other end," Karl nodded in the opposite direction. "Come on, children," he motioned Pete and Jenna to him. With Frieda's arm tucked in his, Karl took his family away to their car.

Jenna waved at Alex. "See you tomor—rowwww!" she sang out in a high voice.

I rolled my eyes.

Alex smiled and waved back. Our family turned and ambled back to the van. Alex walked in the lead, followed by me, then Mom and Dad.

"Pretty nice concert, right boys?" Mom asked as we neared the van.

"Yes, I thought ... Hey!" Alex stopped in mid-sentence. "Look at those motorcycles parked down this row."

I dashed toward the bikes.

"I bet they're the same ones we saw take off at the Alpenblick this morning," Alex said. "A Ducati and a BMW. Do you remember the license plate numbers?"

"I have the numbers in my backpack." When I reached the motorcycles, I nodded my head. I was sure they were the same bikes. They sat about forty feet from where Dad had parked the van. As I turned toward the van, my eyes popped wide open at the sight. "Hey, Mom and Dad," I called out. "Someone broke into our van."

I ran to the van, which was near the back of the parking lot, next to several paths through the woods. There were only a few other cars left in this part of the parking lot. The back hatch of the Go-Mobile was open. Backpacks, bags, and boxes lay at crazy angles on the ground with food, tools, equipment, and some clothing strewn about.

"Hello." A white haired man three rows over waved at us.

"Hello." I waved back.

"Do you need assistance?" The man's wife let go of her door and peered intently through the dim light. "Have you been robbed?"

The couple walked over to see if they could help.

"Incredible! This must have just happened," Dad said after racing to the van. He pulled his right hand through his hair. "I'm calling the Polizei."

"Yes. Do that. This is highly unusual in this area," the elder gentleman agreed.

I bent down to see under the van, checking under the seats. "Dad, where are the dogs? They're not under or in the car."

Alex ran to the edge of the parking lot, calling for Thunder.

Mom finally got to the van. "Honey," she said, almost in tears, "I don't see any police right now. We need to make sure everything is all still here."

"Can we help in any way?" The older German woman came over to Mom and stood near her.

"Maybe. Let us see if anything is missing first." Mom rubbed her eyes.

"Alex, come back and make sure we have everything," Dad said.

Alex gave up on calling the dogs and helped with the search of the stuff strewn all over the ground. We picked up the clothes and equipment, stuffing it back into the bags and boxes within fifteen minutes. Dad had Alex and me load the stuff back into the van. We crawled into our back seat area and made sure our backpacks were all right. Nothing was missing—except the dogs.

"Everything's here," Mom said. "All our information, money, food. Nothing's been taken."

Alex and I both nodded our heads in agreement.

"Well, I'm going to ensure whoever did this gets caught and pays for breaking and entering," Dad said.

"That is the right thing to do," said the German gentleman.

"Honey," Mom said, dabbing at wetness around her eyes. "How? How are you going to do anything when there aren't any policemen here?" She walked over to her passenger seat and sat down pressing her hanky with both hands to catch the tears. "At least my jewelry wasn't here. And what about the dogs?"

Dad went over to talk with Mom while Alex and I stood by the back of the van with our backpacks. I turned away from Mom and Dad and saw the bikes. "We've got to do something to get the dogs back."

"Sir," the white haired man spoke up. "If you like, I'll walk with you to find the Polizei. My wife can stay here with yours to keep her company."

"Thanks," Dad said as he walked past us. "Let's find a policeman." He turned to Mom, "Honey, why don't you start the van to warm up a bit and chat with this man's wife. I'll be back in a few minutes."

The door clicked shut and the engine started as the men walked away. Mom and the German woman were in the front seats of the van.

I pulled my morning notes out of my backpack. "Those motorcycles have the same license plates we saw this morning: MLM-993 and DSC-334."

"Maybe Thunder and Lightning scared the biker dudes off?" Alex said.

The minute Alex finished talking, the faraway sound of dogs barking broke the silence.

"That's Thunder, I know his bark!" Alex declared.

"And that's Lightning, too," I added. "We need to go see what's happening!"

We grabbed our packs and took out flashlights.

I pulled open the van door. "Mom, Thunder and Lightning sound like they are right over there." I pointed to the edge of the parking lot. "Towards the Poellat Gorge. We'll get them and come back."

"Oh no, you don't," she said.

"We'll find Dad first," Alex said.

"Stay in this parking lot until you talk with your dad," Mom said.

"Okay," I agreed. "Let's go!"

We ran in the direction Dad had gone. We saw him standing next to the friendly German talking to a cop near the road. His loud voice carried well in the quieter night air. Waving his hands, he kept moving back and forth, nodding and shaking his head. As we got nearer, the cop handed him some papers.

"Dad, we heard the dogs. We need to go to the Poellat Gorge," Alex said when we were near enough to be heard. "Mom said we had to tell you."

"Okay," Dad said. "I'll be done here in a few minutes." The policeman had Dad look at another piece of paper and gave him a pen to fill it out.

I could still hear the dogs barking, but fainter. "Dad, if we don't go now, we won't be able to find them," I said. I couldn't tell if he nodded at the cop or me. "Okay, we'll see you," I yelled, as I turned and flew toward the path that led to the gorge. Alex hesitated as I ran past, then caught up to me.

The hair on the back of my neck was standing up as our arms and legs strained to move us faster. I turned on my flashlight as we hit the mountain trail. *I'm not afraid,* I told myself quickly, *I'm alert.* I repeated this several times under my breath as my feet pounded the dirt trail, ducking to avoid low branches near the path.

THE MOONLIT
CHASE

As we reached the bottom of the gorge, we stopped to listen and look. A few hundred yards in front of us, two silhouettes dashed through a clearing and disappeared around a bend in the moonlit Poellat Gorge trail. Not far behind them, we heard our dogs giving chase.

We lost them as we raced into the trees toward the narrow bend, where the cascading water drowned out any other sound. My clothes felt damp from the spray and I could see steam rising from the stream's surface. As we made the turn, the moonlight shone brightly through scattered clouds. Between tree limbs, I saw two figures rapidly climbing the rocky part of the gorge. Thunder and Lightning's barks bounced off the rocks and water, echoing through the night. As we trailed them, the hoodlums paused at irregular intervals, each swinging something at the dogs to keep them away. Tree limbs blocked my sight enough so that I couldn't make out what they were using to strike at the dogs. Each time they stopped to fight back the dogs, we closed some of the distance between us.

"Man, they are moving fast," I said, panting a bit.

"They must know the area." Alex said before jumping onto a small boulder.

"Stay out of the water tonight," I smiled as I leaped from rock to rock. "Temp's a bit colder than in the daytime."

"Quit joking." He sucked in some air and kept moving. "This could be dangerous. I can't see those guys that well, but I think they're heading toward the cave we found earlier."

After we cleared the stream, I stopped and leaned against a tree. "I'm glad you marked the entrance before we left." I took a deep breath. Sweat was starting to run down the middle of my back.

"Me too. But I think the dogs will show us right where it is." Alex paused and wiped some sweat off his forehead and crouched to stretch his legs.

"Did you bring your black light?" I said between puffs of air.

"Of course," Alex's voice sounded confident. "I am so-o-o glad I marked the entrance with invisible black light ink. Even in this semi-darkness, the cave entrance will light up pretty easily."

"That cave should be about halfway between Mary's Bridge and the parking lot and on the left side of the gorge as we climb up." I pushed away from the tree. "We have to keep moving to catch up."

"Right." Alex wiped his forehead again and stood up.

Stones clattered into the stream twenty feet behind us. Alex moved behind a boulder and I hid behind a tree. Dad appeared on the trail two seconds later, sending more stones into the stream.

"You can come out," Dad said. "But keep your talking quieter next time. You're well past the stream's rapids. I overheard you with no problem. That was pretty smart, marking the cave entrance with black light paint to find it easily again."

"Alex marked some of the main passage as well," I added. "We thought it would be fun to come back some time, but not like this." I started to edge forward, but Dad grabbed my right forearm.

"Wait," he said. "How much further to this cave?"

I looked at Alex and shrugged my shoulders.

"I think we still have another quarter of a mile," Alex said.

"Okay. Let me plan what we need to do," Dad said. "First, I need some batteries for my flashlight." He waved his fading light toward the sound of the barking dogs.

"I think I have some." I fished two out of my backpack and handed them to Dad. While we waited, Alex's flashlight beam shot out in front of us, raking the ground to find the quickest way up to the cave.

"Thanks," Dad said. With his shoulder resting on a tree, he reloaded his batteries and thought out loud. "We don't know enough yet. Don't get close to those crooks. Stay away from them and we'll call the dogs back." Screwing his flashlight back together, he gave the orders. "Let's go. Scouts out!"

Alex and I sprinted ahead. Dad kept close behind us. Alex took the lead scout role, moving ahead of me. *Just like an Army scout,* my brain worked at full tilt. *Take a quick look at the situation and report back.*

Thunder and Lightning were now making less noise. I found a quicker way to move up the hill and hurried past Alex, trying to put light on the dogs

Seventy feet in front of me, with their eyes flashing in my light, the dogs darted in and out between two men. The men held up their hands to shield their eyes from being blinded by Alex's and my flashlight beams. Both men were swinging something that looked like a piece of pipe at the dogs. Lunging back and forth, Thunder and Lightning kept working at getting closer to the men.

Suddenly, one of the men vanished.

"I bet he went into the cave," Alex yelled from his position behind a boulder. "I guess we don't need the black light now."

"The other guy's right behind him," I directed my light at him from where I stood behind a pine tree.

The second man vanished from sight as well.

"Okay, scouts." Dad caught up again. "What's the situation?"

Thunder and Lightning began to really raise a ruckus, making all types of barking sounds. Thunder howled out in a deep voice. Lightning's constant yapping interrupted the howls.

"Be quiet!" My voice's frustration carried over the fifty feet from where I was hiding to the dogs. Thunder and Lightning became silent. They swiveled their heads around, located Alex, Dad, and me, then backed away from the entrance of the cave to join our group. I pulled Lightning close and hugged him tight.

"Great work, Thunder," Alex said as he pounded his approval on Thunder's side.

"Awesome job, Lightning." I loosened up enough on my hug to ruffle his longhaired head.

Dad came over and patted each dog on the head. Tails wagging and tongues hanging out, the dogs started looking back at the cave.

"Here's the situation down the hill," Dad explained. "After I realized you two had sprinted off, I took the Polizei officer to your mother to talk about this, then ran after you. She'll need help from me to convince the police to come up here. I don't want these two crooks to get away. I don't want you in danger either." Dad looked around and pointed to some thick brush around a boulder pile. "If I leave you two with the dogs to guard the cave entrance, that should keep the criminals inside. Can you stay behind that pile of rocks with the dogs and not go inside the cave?"

"Dad, they probably ran away," I said. "The cave is like tour caves in the 'States.'"

"Gabe, we don't know the whole situation. If these criminals rifled through our baggage and didn't take anything, there's something odd happening. Don't go after them while I'm away. They seem to be running away, which is the only reason I'm leaving you here. If I can't trust you to stay out of the cave, I'll have to take you down the hill."

"Okay, okay," I gave in. "We won't try to catch them."

"You are to hide, then run back to the van if these two hoodlums come out of the cave," Dad said. He hesitated before he left. "One more thing. Even though you're both in great shape and have been trained in martial arts, you're much younger than them. You're not as strong and you aren't trained to handle crooks, in spite of the fact that I did train you to do a little detective work. They may be more dangerous than you think they are."

I could hear crickets chirping and the wind rustling in the pines, elms, and oaks. The faint light of the moon and glow from the flashlights gave Dad's face shadows that creased his brow. His jaw was tense and his lips were drawn in a straight line as he said, "Seriously, stay away from the cave while I'm gone and keep yourselves out of sight. Let Thunder and Lightning guard the entrance and protect you. If they notice something, let them check it out. Always keep the dogs between you and those crooks. You two stay hidden."

Alex and I both nodded our heads. "Okay, Dad."

Why is Dad super cautious? I tried to be logical. *These two guys are probably young punks playing a prank. What connection did they have with the third guy from the restaurant this morning? He didn't look that sinister. Was he involved? And why would these guys be after our van? There must be a secret they wanted.* My stomach had tightened up and my eyes and ears strained to catch any sign of the men.

Chapter 18

STRIKE THREE: YOU'RE OUT

The dogs were lying on the ground fifty feet from the entrance of the cave, and Thunder was the first to react. He rolled from his side to his feet in a second. His ears perked up.

"What is it, boy?" Alex asked.

Thunder's nose was up in the air. He began sniffing and moving a little closer to the cave. Lightning watched, sniffing the air as well. He followed Thunder toward the cave.

I spied through the crease between two rocks, rubbing the goose bumps on my arms in the cool air. I thought about pulling my jacket out of my backpack, but watched Thunder instead.

Alex's light followed Thunder's progress. He sniffed the air again, letting his tongue hang out. Then he licked his lips several times.

"Oh, you smell food?" Alex said. He looked at his watch. "Past your dinnertime. You must be hungry."

Thunder looked back at Alex.

"Don't go any closer to the cave," Alex pushed his hand out to emphasize his command.

Thunder whined, lying flat on his belly.

"Thunder, stop bellyaching," Alex said. He pointed left and to the front of me with his free hand. "Gabe, look where Lightning is."

Following his direction, I saw a light-colored blob in the moonlight inching forward, half-hidden behind some rocks. I swung my flashlight around and caught Lightning low crawling on his belly about ten feet from the cave.

"Yep. I see him." I stood up and walked to Lightning, tapping him on the nose to halt his progress.

"Alex, we've been waiting at least twenty-five minutes. Dad should be back by now." Tired of waiting, I wanted something to do. *Sitting here is killing me.*

"Yeah. I wonder where he could be." Alex scanned the gorge path with his flashlight. "Maybe he's having trouble getting the Polizei. Do you remember what those two guys we were chasing looked like?"

"Not really, but they didn't look so tough. They were only a little taller than we are." I raised my left hand a little higher than my head.

"Yeah, I agree," Alex said. "With the two dogs keeping them occupied, we should be able to defend ourselves and run if we have to …" Alex's voice trailed off. His head swung to the right and he shifted position as though he saw something.

I looked to the right too. Thunder had been moving closer to the cave, inch by inch. His black bulk was hard to spot in the sporadic moonlight. His head stretched forward as he continued sniffing toward the cave. He had covered most of the distance between the tunnel entrance and us.

Alex said, "Thunder, you're not allowed in the cave. Since you're not listening, I'll have to put you on a leash." Alex strode over to Thunder and clicked his leash into place. He was three feet away from the entrance of the cave. "I don't know what you smell, but I'll feed you later."

I looked down at my feet. Lightning wasn't there. After a few seconds, I spotted him on the opposite side of the approach to the cave, concealing his small body by the bigger rocks and boulders.

Thunder's disobedience had created enough of a distraction for Lightning to sneak closer to the cave.

"Lightning, behave," I said.

His head pivoted to the sound of my voice. Then he stood up, sniffing the ground and moving left and right. He walked back towards me as if the cave didn't attract him at all. When I picked him up to keep him from going back towards the cave, a thought flashed through my mind. *Maybe Alex and I can help Dad and the police before they arrive. Dad said not to go into the cave, but maybe the dogs could sniff out the area.*

"Alex," I said in a low voice, "we need to do something. It's been half an hour now. We haven't heard anything from those crooks. They're probably gone. And the dogs smell something inside. Maybe the dogs can protect us and guard the cave better if they check out whatever's making them hungry."

Alex brought Thunder near me and whispered. "No, we can't go inside. We've been in trouble this whole trip! We've already had Strike One and Two. I don't want Strike Three. Mom and Dad will ground us forever!" Alex sat down and asked Thunder to lay down next to him.

"We're wasting time," I said. "I bet the crooks are getting away. That was a pretty big cave."

"But there may be a way …" Alex thought out loud, "Dad said if Thunder and Lightning detected something, they could investigate. Right?" Without waiting for a reply, he continued, "Then Dad said Thunder and Lightning should defend us. With both dogs on leashes, they can take a quick look inside, make sure we are safe, and we can pull them right back to us. That's defending us. But we have to keep the dogs between us and the crooks."

Alex completely left out the fact that Dad had told us to stay hidden, but I didn't care. I hated sitting around. I jumped to my feet.

"Yeah, that makes sense. Because the dogs smell something wrong, they should investigate. And they'll be between us and those thieves we're tracking." I set Lightning down, leaned over, and clicked his leash in place. "Hey, since Lightning is the lightest, we should let him go in first."

"Okay," Alex sighed. He put Thunder on his leash and told me, "Go!"

We covered the distance to the cave in a minute or so, taking advantage of big rocks for temporary hiding places. No movement or sound came from the cave. The moon briefly peeked out from behind a cloud, then vanished, leaving us with only pale starlight. We peered closely at the cave entrance, but nothing broke the silence except for the background noise of the stream. With a few short instructions to Lightning, I let him go in half the length of his leash and then pulled him back. Nothing. Alex moved me aside and did the same with Thunder. Still no problems.

Thunder and Lightning wagged their tails, danced around our feet, and nuzzled our faces as we crouched down to pet them. The moon broke out from behind the cloud cover. In the moonlight, I could see the dogs' ears perk up as they strained on their leashes toward the cave.

"Still think there's something good in there?" I said to Lightning in a hushed tone as I got him ready to go three-quarters the length of the leash.

Lightning went in first, followed by Thunder. Both went into and came out of the cave without finding anything.

"Good work. You came right back." I rubbed Lightning's head between his ears when he was out. "One last time. Dad says, 'The third time's a charm.' We'll see."

The third time, Alex and I decided to let the dogs go in together. I leaned my already cold chest up against an even colder rock wall at the cave entrance. Lightning and Thunder both tugged on their leashes strongly enough to yank our arms into the cave entrance. Next, Alex almost fell into the cave and I felt a strong jerk on my arm. Both leashes went slack.

Alex backed away from the cave, rapidly gathering Thunder's leash.

"Alex, what's happening?" My blood started pumping. I yanked Lightning's leash back toward me. With half the leash coiled at my feet, the leather became taut again. I gave the rope a twitch to signal Lightning to return.

Alex braced his legs against the rock wall, crouched over, and strained with all his might—only to fall back on the boulders behind him as Thunder's leash went slack once more.

In a few seconds, Thunder and Lightning trotted out of the tunnel, dropping something beside the entrance.

Grabbing my best friend, I rubbed his head against my cheek then held him at arms length. "What were you doing?"

Alex had Thunder sitting. "Thunder, you know better than to drag me into the cave."

After a few words, I set Lightning down. He headed back toward the cave entrance. Thunder jerked away from Alex, running toward Lightning. Lightning sped up, dashing to the cave opening first, picking up something dark. Thunder latched on one end and both dogs growled, flipping their heads one way and then the other to get sole possession of the prize. In a few seconds, the prize ripped into two pieces. Lightning came over to me and lay on the ground, gnawing on something.

"What do you have?" I said, picking up a piece of warm meat and bone.

Thunder was munching, crunching, and swallowing his share of the prize.

"Hey, spit that out Thunder." Alex tried to take control of the situation. "You could be eating something poisonous." Alex grabbed what was left and looked it over with his flashlight. "This steak must be what drew them into the cave. I can feel a little warmth which means someone cooked this less than an hour ago."

"Alex," I said, brushing against Lightning, "Now we *have* to go into the cave. Dad left forty-five minutes ago. There's been no sign of those guys and the dogs might have stolen their dinner. I bet we could sneak in, do a quick recon, and come right back. The dogs had no trouble."

Alex hesitated. "Alright, alright," he said with reluctance. "We need to make sure this steak wasn't someone's dinner. This might help with the investigation if we look at the evidence before the trail gets too cold. But we have to keep the dogs between those crooks and us. We must be fast and we can't go in far." Alex looked over his shoulder, down the moonlit gorge. "Dad should have been back by now."

I followed his gaze. No Dad in sight. No Polizei. *Could be risky,* my inner voice nagged me, *but if we can help Dad, he'd be proud of us for pressing on.*

I decided the crooks must have been pretty dumb. I put my backpack on. "Those idiots in the cave must be gone. T&L didn't meet anyone or they would have been all over them." I slashed my hand through the air with a Karate chop.

"Whatever. Let's get this over with. Keep the dogs on leashes." Alex said as he shrugged on his backpack and moved to the cave entrance. Standing aside, he said, "Gabe, you and Lightning go first."

Flashlight on, I sent Lightning in first and followed right behind him. He had gone in about fifteen feet when he stopped. Thunder, who had squeezed past me to stand right next to him, froze, then sniffed the air. Alex brushed my right shoulder.

"Alex, look ahead." I poked him in the side with my elbow and used my flashlight to show him what I had found. The light glinted off a metal stake in the ground three feet away—tip visible sticking though the center of a big piece of cooked meat.

"That's within the reach of the dogs' leashes." Alex crouched down and spoke to the two dogs. "What's wrong, boys? Don't you want more steak?" Alex turned toward me. "This might be a trap." He got up and started back towards the entrance.

I kept going forward to the stake. I looked closely at the meat and smelled it. "I can't tell if anything is wrong with this meat or not."

The dogs sniffed the air and the sides of the cave as they moved toward the stake.

"Gabe, that doesn't mean anything." Alex came back to the stake, taking a closer look. "Is your nose a chem lab? We've got to go."

Lightning came to me and lay on the ground. Alex's light tracked Thunder, who showed signs of slowing down. With tail drooping, head hung down, and ears relaxed, he moseyed around the area.

"You boys look a little sleepy." I leaned down and patted Lightning's head.

Thunder started going past the stake with Alex in tow, then made a crazy lurch to the right. Lightning's eyes closed for a nap.

"Hey, guys." I pulled on Lightning's leash. "What's wrong?" My sixth sense alarm started going off. I stood up and swung my light around the cave.

Alex's flashlight flicked back between the two dogs. "Nuts!" Alex spit out. "I think the dogs were drugged. Dad will be furious. Quick! We have to get out of here before something else happens." Alex kicked the cave floor in frustration.

"Yeah." I looked down, yanking on the leash to pull Lightning up and get him moving.

Alex walked over to Thunder, picking up his rear end and pushing him back towards the cave entrance.

"Come on!" I said to both dogs. They had settled down on the cave floor. I picked up Lightning while Alex pulled on Thunder's chest to get him moving. With me in the lead, we headed back to the cave entrance, crouching to clear the ceiling as we got near the fresh air flowing in the cave.

Good, I breathed deeply. *Five feet to go.*

A low electric hum cut through the silence. Rapid movement of a huge rock wall in front of the cave entrance cut off the exit. I darted forward. My heartbeat sped up. *We're trapped!*

I heard a clunk and jumped as Alex's limp body hit my back left shoulder, twisted, then dropped to the ground. I dropped Lightning and squeezed next to the rock wall on the right. My light focused on an unconscious Alex as Thunder sniffed him and flopped down, muzzle resting on Alex's chest. Someone had knocked him out.

My heart pounded. Chest heaving, I pumped my fists. No more starlight or fresh air. I listened. Silence. I looked around. Nothing. Alex—a crumpled heap in near total darkness—was still breathing. Lightning dragged himself from where I had dropped him. He curled up next to Thunder. I bent over Alex to get a better look.

Without warning, I saw a galaxy of stars exploding in the sky. I felt myself sink to the ground before I blacked out.

Chapter 19

THE LION'S DEN

I swam back to consciousness. Letting out a long moan, I squeezed my eyes tightly to get rid of the pain surging throughout my body. After a few minutes, I squinted my eyes, opening them for a moment without seeing anything. *My head, my head!* Throbbing, shooting pains stabbed me when I moved my head, especially to the right. Without touching it, I felt tenderness on the upper right side of my skull.

The cave … we were in the cave … walking … dogs slowing down … panicking … I forced myself, through the pain, to remember what happened. *This might be the same cave we started in, but …* I focused a little harder in the dim light filtering in from a sliver of space where a door stood slightly ajar. *What's a door doing in a cave?* I didn't recognize anything. I rested my eyes. When I opened them again, I saw dark shapes several feet away. Willing my eyes to clear, I stared longer. Soon, I could see the dark shapes moving with a regular rise and fall. I could make out the outline of Lightning's head. *Must be Thunder and Lightning piled together.*

A heavy, deep snore that had to be Thunder's broke the silence. A lighter, higher fluttery sound joined in. "Snuk ... snuk ... snuk," came from Thunder in a steady low-pitched rhythm with Lightning's higher, more airy "Whee ... oooh ... oooh ... eee." *The dogs are okay.* I smiled and immediately regretted it as a sharp pain ran down the side of my face.

Despite occasional fiery darts in my neck and an exploding headache, I raised my head, peering left and right around the room. *No one here. Good. Now where am I?* I continued to squint to get my bearings. *Man, this headache is killing me.* I let my head sink back to the ground. I felt numb. I tried to move my right hand to touch my head. No success. My hands were tied behind me. When I pulled with my hands, a thousand needles stabbed into my skull and I felt a tug on my legs. *My wrists must be tied to my feet. I can't believe we're trapped!* I sucked in a deep breath as that fact sunk in. In no time, a feeling of helplessness washed over me. Tears started welling up in my eyes.

Stop feeling sorry for yourself. You are not a quitter, I mentally prodded myself. Despite the rush of pain and numbness in my arms, I rolled and looked to my left, barely making out another form on the ground. Even in the poor light I could see the figure had dark hair. Steeling myself against the stabbing pain, I moved my head a little higher. It was Alex.

We were lying several feet apart. I gritted my teeth and strangled any painful yells as I wiggled over the jagged floor toward him, pausing to listen for our kidnappers. Shoulder, hips, knees, hips, shoulders. Broken stalagmites and little sharp, gravelly stone pieces littered the floor. Sharp pinpricks ripped into me from my head, my side, shoulder, and hips. Deep breathing and muffled grunts punctured the quiet. *Halfway there. Rest. Fight the pain.* I stopped a foot away.

Alex was lying on his left side, facing away from me. I pulled my knees forward to give Alex a pretty good jolt in the legs, but my knees barely brushed him because of the way the crooks had tied me. Alex didn't move. I squirmed to within three inches of his body, clothes continuing to rustle while rubbing the cavern floor. I paused, then used my whole body, and gave Alex another big knee jab. This time Alex's legs jerked away.

Wake-up! I screamed in my head, but didn't let out a sound.

Alex rolled his right side into me. I dug my shoulder into the ground and squirmed backward. Alex finished rolling onto his back. He turned his head toward me, eyelids barely opening. The weak light cast my shadow over him. I saw his cheeks drawn up to his eyes in a grimace of pain. The outline of a large lump on the left side of his head caused me to wonder if the right side of my head looked the same.

"Gabe," Alex croaked out at me, "What happened?" He gritted his teeth as he spoke and closed his left eye.

"We've been kidnapped," I whispered through clenched teeth. "I don't see the jerks that did this to us, but we have to get free from these cords around our hands and feet."

"Gabe, do you hear that snoring coming from over there?" Alex mumbled as if in shock. "What is it?"

"Thunder and Lightning are singing a duet," I said sarcastically. "Now, focus …" I hissed, still fighting the pain in my head.

"Ha, ha, ohhhhh!" Alex slammed his eyelids shut and his lips tightened. Then he said, "These ropes are killing my hands. How can we get them off? I bet your hands are tied up like mine, behind your back."

I thought for a minute. "Roll on your left side." I stared at Alex's hands and feet. His wrists were tied together behind his back. The cords were about a half-inch thick and wrapped tightly, cutting into his skin. His ankles were also cinched tight, and a small, short cord tied the wrist and ankle ropes together. I yanked my hands up again and my feet moved. *I'm tied up just like Alex.* I couldn't straighten up all the way or move my hands too far from my back.

"Here's what we can do," I said. "I'll roll onto my right side so we'll be back to back. I'll try to untie you." I groaned out loud as I rolled and moved closer to him, scraping my side again on the cave floor.

"Gabe, no sounds," Alex whispered forcefully. "Keep going. Whoever tied us up might be close."

Crushing stones and gravel into my body, I scooted even closer, stopping and listening for the crooks.

"Hurry," Alex said.

"I'm getting there. Don't rush me!" A few more minutes passed until I was close enough to touch Alex's ropes. I flexed my numb fingers, trying to get feeling back. Untying knots was easy at home. *This should be a cinch.* I began working the knot loose.

After five minutes, Alex said, "Something wrong?"

"I thought this would be easy, but it's hard to move any part of the rope," I said.

"We don't have a lot of time."

"I know. I'm working." I clenched my jaw as my fingers worked to pull the ropes apart. Like steel chains welded together, they wouldn't budge.

I dug harder with my fingernails. I could feel them pull back from my fingers and something wet trickled onto my right hand. *Must be bleeding.* After what seemed like forever and with lots of brotherly encouragement, there was some movement in the knots.

At that instant, the door hinge screeched and the door scraped against the floor of the cave. Faded yellow light spilled into the room. Someone's voice called out in German as the door swung wide.

I froze. Fear tingled down my spine.

"Gabe, get back to where you started." Alex's hoarse whisper slashed through my panic.

I wiggled away from Alex as fast as possible, fighting the pain as rock chips dug into my side once again. The extra light let me see we were in a room carved out of rock.

On the other side of the door, two male voices spoke in guttural tones. One of the men, laughing loudly, entered the room. He was a dark-haired, young man dressed in a dark blue coveralls and heavy boots. He carried a small kerosene lantern, which he placed on the table in the center of the room. He pointed to different corners of the room, speaking in German. The basic German we had studied let me understand some of the simple words he used.

The blond-haired kidnapper leaned over Alex, who stiffened.

I glared at the enemy. My eyes had cleared enough for me to recognize Blondie as one of the young 'biker-dudes' from the Alpenblick Gasthaus. I took in every detail of the man as he lifted Alex.

I swallowed hard when Blondie dumped Alex on the floor and turned around to come toward me. *Blondie, you're not going to get away with this!* Putting his arms under my knees and my back, he picked me up a few feet off the ground, then he dropped me like a sack of potatoes.

"Ungh!" flew out of my mouth. Starry lights swirled as my head bounced against the rock floor.

Blondie checked the ropes around my wrists and ankles. He must have been satisfied because he rolled me onto my back. In the opposite corner of the room, I watched the dark-haired kidnapper check Alex's ropes. *They must not want us next to each other,* I guessed. A silent sigh escaped my lips. The kidnapper didn't notice I had loosened Alex's ropes a little. Blondie grabbed my ropes and dragged me even farther away from Alex to an opposite corner. I barely kept my head off the cave floor. Tears fell to the ground as the gravel scraped and punctured my skin.

The hoodlums began talking in German again, but seemed to disagree about something. Raising his voice, one of them pounded on the table. The dark-haired man balled his fists. He moved toward Blondie and leaned forward. While the argument heated up, I used the time and extra light to size up our "living quarters." The cave room was a medium-sized room. The ceiling would have been twenty-feet high, except that massive stalactites extended down for about twelve feet, leaving only eight feet of clearance from the floor. I calculated our room was almost fifteen feet wide and twenty feet long.

The soft yellow light was bright enough to make out the black and orangish-red shapes of Thunder and Lightning lying in the right hand corner of the room—the side with the door. Alex and I were lying next to the wall across from the entryway. The two men had placed me at the left end of the twenty-foot room, away from the dogs and Alex. I took a quick look at sides of the cave.

They were hewn out of the gray rock that contained a few crystals. *No easy escape route through the walls.* The gravel and loose stone scrunched under the boots of our captors as they moved around. Some unbroken stalagmites still thrust up from the floor in the corners of the room. The rocky walls were uneven, but much smoother than the floor of the cave.

The men finally calmed down. The dark-haired man in blue coveralls spoke in broken English.

"You American boys lay still or we come back and punish. You try to escape and we beat you." With added emphasis he pounded on the table, making my body involuntarily jerk at the sound. He adjusted his blue coveralls and grabbed the kerosene lantern. The burning wick was starting to smoke, putting out a strong kerosene smell. I looked past the men walking out the door and glimpsed an even larger cavern, which also seemed brighter. Blondie blocked my view as he shut the door, leaving us in pitch-black darkness.

"Alex," I said, "We need to get out of here now."

"Let's wait just a minute to ensure those guys don't come right back," Alex cautioned. "You know the dark-haired man was one of those biker-dudes from the hotel."

"Yeah, I know," I said. "So was the guy who picked me up. They looked younger in the hotel—about nineteen, I think."

After counting to sixty in my head, I began moving toward Alex again.

"I can't see anything, but I memorized our positions when I could see by the lantern's light." I grimaced again. "My headache's like a dagger and the pounding makes it hard to think. How are you?" I winced as I dragged myself closer to Alex.

"My head is killing me. Let's move together. You can untie me."

"Already moving, old chap," I said with a British accent, remembering a World War I movie where badly wounded soldiers kept going. I could hear rustling from Alex's progress. We reached the table at about the same time.

"I'm ready," Alex said.

"Roger, dodger." Again I maneuvered my body close enough to touch Alex's hands, flipped onto my right side, and continued untying the knots, with my back next to Alex's.

"My headache is going away a little," I said in spite of the stinging shocks and throbbing pulses. "Hard to focus. But I'm not quitting."

"Mine hasn't stopped at all," Alex said. "When we get these ropes off, I'm taking some Tylenol out of my first aid kit."

In twenty minutes, I had unraveled the last knot. Now Alex's hands were free.

"Man that feels good," he said.

I waited a few seconds. "What are you doing, Alex? I'm still tied up. Get me out of these ropes."

"I'm rubbing my wrists to get the circulation going so I can feel my fingers," Alex said. "My wrists are sticky. The cords must have made them bleed."

"Don't take forever," I said while rolling on my back. It was hard to wait patiently while looking at inky blackness. Without saying a word, Alex rolled me back on my side and untied my wrists. I sat up, working with as much speed as possible to free my ankles.

"We have to move fast," Alex said. "We know those idiots could be back any moment."

I reached out into nothingness to find Alex. As soon as I touched him, I grabbed his shoulder. With the other hand I found the table and pulled myself to my feet. I held onto the edge for balance, listening to Alex stand up. We paused to get our bearings. Only the drugged snores from our "invincible" watchdogs interrupted the silence.

"Let's get the dogs up," Alex said.

"Right," I said. "Then, we need to get out of here. Where can we go?"

"Deeper into the cave," Alex said, bumping into me before I heard his feet crunching towards the right side of the room.

"What are you doing?" I asked.

"I'm getting on my knees, looking for our backpacks," Alex said. "I thought they were right next to where the blond-haired guy dumped me."

"Oh, okay. I remember something heaped up next to Thunder and Lightning."

Neither the poor lighting from the kerosene lamp nor the earlier light leaking in past the cracked door had been bright enough for me to see all the details of the room. I heard Alex's hand brushing on the floor close to Thunder and Lightning—near the short wall on the right side. I decided to help as well, but I was as slow as a tortoise. I extended my hands and waved them in front of me in the dark to avoid running into the wall as I shuffled forward step by careful step. In a minute my palms connected with the cool wall that contained the door. I moved closer to the dogs and knelt down, feeling the gritty floor as I searched. *That pile has to be the backpacks. The kidnappers probably dumped our bags in here.* A moment later I reached the heap I had seen, and whispered, "Alex."

"What?"

"I'm right where I thought the heap was, but it's only a pile of rough blankets. They're probably here because this room is chilly. Feels like there's a vent here somewhere. Maybe the bags are outside the room with those crooks."

Alex let out another big sigh. "All of our survival tools are in those bags. We have to get the bags. We'll have to go through that squeaky door into a well-lit cave. We can't do that without them seeing us." Alex sounded defeated.

"If we work like a tag team, we'd have a better chance."

"Okay," Alex said. I heard him sit on the floor. "You know, we need help," he continued. "We're like the guy in the Bible who the king threw into the lion's den. God rescued him by shutting the lion's mouth."

"This is more like a den of thieves and we're their treasure." I got quiet. "That guy's name was Daniel."

Alex's feet scraped the floor as he moved around. "I think we need to ask God for help."

"Your idea. You ask … you pray."

Alex paused, and then whispered. "God, we messed up big time! We didn't listen to Dad's warnings. We're sorry. We'll listen better next time. Right now, we need your help to get us safely out of this 'lion's den.' Thanks."

"Me, too," I chimed in.

"You're supposed to say 'amen' to end a prayer." Alex corrected me. "So be it."

"Okay, *amen*," I said with intensity. "Now let's get cracking. Since I thought of getting those bags, you hold the door and I'll run into the larger cave. I didn't hear our guards lock the door when they left, did you?"

"Nope. Should be unlocked. You go ahead. But be quiet."

We shuffled to the door, our waving hands colliding in the air. I stayed next to the wall and soon Alex was behind me. The door was easy to identify.

"I've got the handle," Alex said.

My reflex was to nod my head in the dark, but I realized Alex couldn't see me. "I'm right next to the edge of the door," I said. "Go."

A high-pitched creak sounded from rusty hinges. I cringed, waiting for the kidnappers to react. Alex stopped when the door was open a foot wide. A welcome ray of weak light came in. Alex slid behind the door. Closing his eyes, he let out a rapid hissing through his clenched teeth, then he stopped. My heart was pounding in my chest.

Nothing happened. Silence.

Alex cracked his eyelids open and glanced at me. I gave him a thumbs-up. He opened the creaking door wide enough for me to see more. I raised two thumbs.

"Our backpacks are against the far wall, about thirty feet away," I said, leaning my head against the rock wall to see them. "I hope they didn't take our caving gear."

Alex nodded. "We asked God for help. We have to trust we'll get it." He tapped my shoulder. "This is really risky, but if I had to pick anyone to race across a room unseen, I'd pick you."

I put my head outside the door's frame. The larger cavern outside our rocky "lion's den" had no end in sight in either direction as the curving passageway on either side blocked the view. I didn't see anyone in the area. Overhead, low wattage electric lights spaced about twenty feet apart appeared to be the only lighting in the cave, except for the lantern on a side table. Light gray rock walls blended with lighter tan rocks in no apparent pattern. The ceiling of the cave had stalactites, but there were no stalagmites on the floor. The side table had a few wooden folding chairs pushed to the side and on top were flashlights and a few packs of cigarettes.

I looked left, then right, easing my head and shoulders out into the passageway. Nobody was around. Like a silent shadow, I sprinted to the backpacks, grabbed them, and flew back to the door, sliding inside next to Alex.

With the door left open to bring light into our room, we ripped into the backpacks, pulled out our headlamps, and slipped them on.

"Owww, my head!" I said in a loud voice.

"Shhhh!" Alex warned me. "Here. Take this Tylenol with a swig of water from your canteen. Hurry. We have to close the door."

I popped the medicine into my mouth and took a long drink. I closed the wooden door.

The rusty hinges creaked in protest again.

"They need to use WD-40 oil on those hinges," I said, feeling more confident with our backpacks and gear. Darkness surrounded us again. I let the tension out with a big breath of air.

"Don't turn your light on yet," Alex said. "What did you see?"

"We can't use the main cavern to make our getaway because there is too much light. The tunnel's electric lights run in both directions," I said, tightening my headlamp straps. "Besides, the biker-dudes might have gone either way."

"Think. We need to brainstorm to figure another way out." Alex muttered to himself in his typical, logical fashion.

I fought an internal urge to give up. My mind searched for answers, but came up with nothing. "I can't think of anything. What about you?"

Alex didn't hesitate. "Let's check out this room and get the dogs up. Maybe that vent you were talking about is big enough to crawl through and get away."

"Roger," I said.

We both flicked our lights on together. As the beams from our headlamps swept the room, Alex's hand gripped my arm like a steel vise.

Chapter 20

WAY OF ESCAPE

Alex pulled me across the room, opposite the door to the main cavern. I almost fell over, stumbling behind him, failing to pry his fingers off my forearm.

"Alex, let go," I said.

"Look," Alex said as he released my arm. He grabbed one side of a four-foot by eight-foot piece of plywood painted flat black and slid it to the right. Behind the wood was a black wrought iron gate blocking a tunnel. Cool air spilled out of the opening into our room. "Here's our exit!" Alex's low volume did not hide the excitement in his voice.

I tapped the piece of plywood. "This black color blended in perfectly to the wall when I scanned the room earlier," I said. Yanking on the large padlock on the gate, I frowned. "It's locked, genius. How do we get through this?"

"I have a lock-picking kit in my bag. Came with my detective lessons from last summer. I think this one's simple enough."

"Okay, but be quick. I don't want to get caught again by the biker-dudes." While Alex worked on the lock, I checked out the tunnel. "We'll need a little light to see where we are going in this tunnel—it's a lot smaller than the main cavern."

"Ta da!" Alex smiled as he held up the opened lock. He swung open the gate and threw the lock into the tunnel entrance. "Let's get the dogs."

We turned around. Thunder and Lightning lay against the wall, snoring softly. Next to them were blankets and burlap bags piled in disarray. The table right in front of us was the only other furniture in the room. After a quick survey of the room, we swiveled back to the tunnel. Behind the table and in front of the tunnel, the uneven ceiling sloped down to only a few inches above Alex's head. As the ceiling sloped, the stalactites became shorter, flowing into the smaller tunnel which had a smooth, but uneven ceiling. The tunnel passageway was about four feet across and extended for about fifteen feet, then appeared to continue to the left.

"Not too promising," I said.

"I'll lead," Alex moved around the table. We normally argued over who went first, but not this time. We had to hurry.

"I'll grab Thunder," Alex said. "You pick up Lightning. Let's move!"

I grabbed Alex's shoulder as he moved to get Thunder. "We've been loose for more than an hour. Those crooks could be back any minute. We should work in the dark if we can."

"No problem—let's switch the lights off as soon as I'm in front of the tunnel."

Alex hurried to the corner where the dogs lay and threw Thunder over his shoulders in a fireman's carry. Then he lumbered back to the opening, bending under the weight of Thunder's bulky body.

"Lights off," Alex said as I took my position right behind him while carrying Lightning.

"Wait," I said. "I'm locking this gate. If the kidnappers chase us, this should slow them down." I picked up the lock, swung the gate closed, and closed the lock, pulling down on it and pushing the gate to double-check. "Okay, lights off."

Remembering earlier pitch-dark caving exercises with Dad, I stretched out my right hand to touch Alex's back to stay in contact. Instead of his back, I felt Thunder's soft fur underneath my fingertips.

Alex moved slowly in silence. I felt Thunder's weight shift as Alex leaned left and right to steady himself. He whispered, "We've reached the corner."

"Move faster. Turn your light on. I want to see what's next."

"My thoughts exactly," Alex said.

Alex flicked on his light, illuminating the passage. I tried to see around Thunder and Alex, but they blocked my view. Two seconds later, the light went out.

"Not good," Alex said. "It looks like there's forty feet of straight passageway that dead-ends. And the tunnel looks smaller at the end, maybe only about three feet wide and five feet tall."

"Are you sure it's a dead end?" I said. My blood pumped harder and my voice got louder.

"We'll see," Alex said. "Don't get concerned yet. We won't know until we get there. And keep your voice down if you're worried about the kidnappers. These tunnels probably carry sounds for long distances." Talking out loud, Alex analyzed the number of steps he would have to take to reach the end of the tunnel, ending with, "... thirteen steps should do it."

I felt Thunder's muzzle moving up Alex's back. "What are you doing?" I asked.

"The cave ceiling is getting lower. I have to carry Thunder in front." Alex grunted, then shifted his backpack. "Let's go."

Alex took his first step to move forward, with me right behind him.

A great idea hit me. "Stop," I said. I set Lightning down, took out a flexible glow-in-the-dark stick from a side pocket in my backpack, bent it until the inside capsule snapped, and shook it hard. A greenish glow broke through the darkness. I tied the stick to Alex's backpack with its outside pocket strings that had been tucked away. *There. Now I have some light, but the glow doesn't travel too far. It definitely won't be seen by anyone around the corner behind us.* I congratulated myself.

"Hey! Turn the light out," Alex said.

"It's a glow stick," I said in the eerie green glow. "There's not too much light and our bodies will block most of it from going behind us."

"Well, get one out for me," Alex said. "Then I can see. I can't get one while I'm holding Thunder."

"Alright, alright," I said. "But you could thank me for a good idea."

"Nice." Alex leaned his back against the left side of the tunnel wall, resting Thunder on his legs and waiting for the glow stick.

I snapped another one, shaking the stick over my head. This time a yellow glow combined with the green glow, making the light less spooky. I tied the stick to his right backpack strap with a short piece of cord to keep his hands free.

"Now, that's better." Alex said.

We covered the remaining thirty feet.

I looked back and couldn't see the turn we had made. "We need to see better," I said. "I'm turning on my light. No one's chasing us yet."

The bright illumination brought the tunnel into focus. I looked at the tan and gray rock wall to the left. The cool breeze in the tunnel flowed out of a two-foot high, triangular-shaped jagged crack that was almost a foot wide at the bottom.

Alex swung his light to the right. "Solid rock to the front and right."

I sank to the ground with Lightning's barely breathing form in my lap. I wrestled to keep my disappointment inside. In a weak voice I said, "We're not gonna make it. We can't escape through that small of a hole."

My high hopes of freedom came crashing down.

Chapter 21

TEST OF COURAGE

Alex set Thunder down and rocked back and forth on his heels, hand on his chin. His headlamp's light moved up and down the right wall. "Let's think this through. The gate we came through wasn't that old and the lock was recently put there. But the biker-dudes said there was no exit from our room. Maybe someone blocked off this pathway for some reason." Alex sat down. "We're stuck."

"It doesn't make sense to me," I objected, my voice wavering. "Why would there be a gate on the tunnel unless there is a way out? There's got to be a secret exit here."

I laid Lightning on the floor of the tunnel, and put my hands and light on the left wall, feeling for a latch of some kind.

"We're way back in a small cave," Alex said. "I know how you feel, but this tunnel doesn't show any signs of recent use."

"Well, what about the cave entrance in the gorge? It was closed by a motor or something, maybe there's a switch to open and close a door here." My voice became steadier. "Let's at least look," I said in exasperation.

"Okay, okay," Alex conceded. "Let's look. Not much else we can do."

We started low, getting on our hands and knees, feeling the rocky surface and looking for anything that might lead us to an opening.

"Hey, Gabe. Come here," Alex said from the right wall. "This wall doesn't look like one piece of rock."

I glanced where the edge of the rock wall joined the jagged stone surface in the front of the tunnel. Too straight to be natural.

Alex poked me to get my attention. "Look to your right."

When I swiveled my head, I saw a strange design carved into the right side of the rock wall near the ceiling, about five feet from where the tunnel stopped. I stood up and tip-toed around the motionless Thunder and Lightning. The design wasn't a family coat of arms or castle crest. It was an X over an old handcart used for mining. My hands rubbed over the symbol, but nothing happened. Disappointed, I looked back at Alex.

"It's a useless mining sign—there's no secret button to push." I leaned against the wall, slid down to the floor next to Lightning, placed one hand on my aching head, and propped my right arm on a small rock ledge a few feet high.

The ledge shifted down a few inches. A slight hum filled the air. Three feet of rock wall on the right slid up into the ceiling, revealing another passageway.

"Yes!" I jumped up and shouted. As the sound echoed off the stone, I clamped my hand over my mouth, imagining the biker's hot breath on the back of my neck. I looked back down the tunnel. The passage remained silent and dark.

I reached out my hand to Alex. He slapped it in a high-five.

"Way to go, bro," Alex said. Without pausing, he pointed his headlamp into the darkness, exposing the side passage. "It's about twenty feet long. Leave your light on. The double bend we've come through will block the light from the kidnappers' view. We should be safe now."

Alex picked up the seventy-five-pound snoring fur-ball and staggered down the new passageway. "Thunder's killing my back.

I can't keep this up too much longer." He came to an abrupt halt three feet from the end, knelt down, and put Thunder on the gravel floor. He stood up, muttering.

"What?" I said as I tried to squeeze forward. I could feel the adrenaline flowing again.

"There's no escape," Alex said. "On the right, there's a tunnel branch with a bunch of rubble and junk from an earlier cave-in, I think. To my front is another rock wall."

I peered over Alex's right shoulder. Several football-sized rocks lay in the main passageway. Piled stones, dirt, and tangled electrical cords covered the side tunnel's floor, rising in the distance until the heap reached the cave's ceiling.

"I wonder what those electrical cords are for." Alex bent down to examine them.

"Probably for lighting for the miner's railcars. See the end of the tracks under that boulder?" I pointed to my right.

"Well, they're of no use now. Besides the blockages up ahead, there's a huge drop-off on my left," Alex continued.

I looked over Alex's left shoulder as best I could, holding Lightning and straining to squeeze forward enough to see. "Looks like it's about a thirty-five to forty-foot drop—I guess we'll have to go down."

"I can't see the other side of the cave." Alex swept his light over the edge.

I got down on my knees to see over the ledge. "The cliff's bottom has a few ten-foot boulders right below us. That might help."

"Yep. We don't have any other choice." Alex kicked the dirt and loose rocks, knocking some over the edge of the cliff. As they clattered down to the base of the drop, he said, "We can't go back, so we have to go forward, I mean ... down."

Frustrated, I set Lightning down and took off my backpack. I unzipped the large outer pocket, pulling out my rope and some karabiner clips. *At least this is something we know how to do.* I thought through each step we had to do to make the descent. *Rappelling safely down this huge drop will take lots of time, time we may not have.* I looked back over my shoulder again, feeling my stomach tighten up.

"How are we going to get Thunder down?" Alex said. "He's too heavy to carry."

"Let's make him a rope harness to support his whole body."

"Good idea. Why don't you make the harness while I start setting up on the wall."

"What? He's your dog."

"Stop whining. I'm better at setting the pitons; you're better at knots."

"Since when? Dad said I did fine on our last climb. And I set the pitons for that."

"Gabe, stuff it. Unless you want me to quit and wait for the bikers right here." Alex sat down facing me, arms crossed.

"You stubborn ..." I picked up my backpack, slamming it against the wall. Dust flew everywhere. A karabiner fell out and rolled off the edge of the cliff, making clicking sounds as it hit bottom.

"Feel better?" Alex raised an eyebrow. "Or do you want to throw more stuff down the cliff?"

"Alright." I hated when he made me mad. "I'll make the harness. But not because you're better than me at setting pitons. I don't want those kidnappers to catch us." I jerked some nylon rope out of my backpack. With furious speed, I made a rope harness that would hold up the front and back parts of Thunder.

The sounds of hammer striking piton echoed in the cavern. Alex pounded pitons in the wall with karabiner rings attached for the rope to run through. We had to risk the noise of setting the pitons, even though the kidnappers might hear us. It was pound or get caught.

"Is that good enough?" I shoved the makeshift harness in front of Alex's nose. He nodded his head.

"Who goes down first?" Alex said as he put Thunder in the harness.

"I'll go." I said. "I'm lighter than you. It'll be easier for you to stop me and pull me back up if necessary."

Alex got in position to belay me. Working together with the skills honed by our years of caving and climbing experience, I clipped my harness onto the rope and got my gear ready as Alex anchored the rope in case he lost his footing.

I placed Lightning in my backpack, leaving his head sticking out of the top. As I did this, he stirred a little.

I whispered into his ear, "Hey buddy, I'm glad you're waking up." I felt better cheering up my groggy friend. After rubbing his longhaired head, I stretched my muscles for the descent. I prepared mentally for going down into an unexplored cavern where we had only estimated the length of the drop. Alex's rope was eighty feet long. Getting one of us down would be no problem because the person keeping the rope from sliding freely was at the top. But when that person was on the bottom, it would take twice the length of the rope to keep the person from falling. If the drop was more than forty feet, one of us would be stuck at the top of the cliff. A shiver ran up my back as I got into position and leaned back over the ledge.

"On belay," Alex stated.

"Going down." I leaned back at a forty-five degree angle. I could feel the harness tighten and felt the backpack with Lightning pulling on my back. Moving my feet one at a time and testing the rock face with each step, I moved slowly down the side of the dark cliff with my light shining on my feet. Twelve feet down, my left foot slipped, sending a crashing storm of little rocks and pieces of the cliff to the bottom. My body jerked in the harness and my face collided with the wall. My lips burned. I tasted blood.

"What happened?"

"The wall goes back underneath a few feet and drops to a ledge," I called back. "Let me down five feet."

Alex lowered me until I got my feet on the ledge. I steadied myself, breathing slowly and leaning into the cliff. The knot in my stomach eased. *Safe again.*

"You okay?" Alex leaned over the edge at the top.

"Except for a fat, bloody lip," I said. I wiped my forearm against my stinging lip, licked the salt taste away, holding it for a minute to stop the bleeding. I felt my aching teeth. *Good. They're alright.* My muscles released their tightness. "I'm going to keep going," I said. Ten minutes later, my stretched-out right foot touched the bottom.

"I'm down," I called, my voice echoing off a distant wall.

"Roger. I'm off belay," Alex said in a loud voice. "I'll get Thunder ready next."

I unhooked from the rope, looked around the base, and pivoted to see where we would go next. My light cut into the inky darkness, finding heaps of stones with some smooth ground. I walked away from the rock wall.

"Gabe, where are you going?" Alex's voice bounced back and forth several times. "I'm lowering Thunder. You're supposed to take care of him as he comes down."

"Oh. Got it." I turned around to walk back. Stalagmites of various heights covered the cavern floor, most of them less than a foot high. The ground rose slightly from the cliff to where I stood. From this angle, I could make out a winding, semi-smooth footpath that had been cleared to the overhang, thirty feet away. I glanced up forty feet to the ledge where Alex was and saw Thunder swinging over the edge of the cliff. I hurried back to the base, watching Thunder moving closer each second.

"Gabe, I hear something behind me," Alex said.

"What is it?"

"Sounds like someone swearing in German. They've found us."

I strained to hear them. Zilch. My mind flashed to a terrible scene of our kidnappers catching us and beating us senseless. My hands clenched. Released.

They're closing in!

Chapter 22

SCHNELL
SPELUNKING

"Alex, get Thunder down here now," I called out.

"I'm not sure I can get him down fast enough."

"He's only about fifteen feet from me. Drop him and I'll catch him."

"You've gotta be kidding me. He's a lot of dead weight," Alex warned.

"Not to worry. I've got him," I insisted.

"Okay," Alex said with a big sigh. Thunder dropped like a black rock. I braced for impact, but Thunder walloped me. Smashed me into the floor. A grunt escaped my lips. Alex's light shone on our tangled bodies.

"Right. I've got him," Alex said "You're lucky I didn't release the rope entirely."

Thunder moaned. He lifted his big slobbery face, tongue hanging out, and smacked me right in the face.

"Eu-yuck!" involuntarily came from my lips. I pushed Thunder off me, rolled to the right and stood up.

"Alex, Thunder's okay," I bellowed.

"Yeah, I see," Alex turned away. "I'm coming down now. The kidnappers are closing in."

I heard snapping sounds as Alex slammed the karabiner clips of his harness around the rope to start down. Thunder leaned his body on my leg, distracting me. Lightning barked to get my attention. He squirmed in the backpack, trying to get out. Thunder wobbled into the cliff face while I stepped over to my backpack.

"It's about time you woke up. Were you dreaming about the tasty meat you ate?" I patted his head. "Stay in the backpack, but get ready. Dreamtime is over and we're on the run." Lightning quit struggling.

"Hey," Alex called down. "You're supposed to belay me."

"Did you drop the rope?"

"On it's way."

"Alex, it's stuck in a cleft. Hurry. Try again!"

Alex tugged several times, got the rope free and dropped it at my feet. I grabbed the rope. "On belay. *Schnell, schnell*. Make it quick."

Alex moved to the edge of the cliff, bending back, executing a rapid rappel down. My headlamp tracked him bouncing off the gray and tan sheer drop in a sea of darkness. He paused halfway to avoid swinging out of control at the cliff face indentation where I split my lip. He kept dropping. Twenty more feet to go.

"Don't stop. There's a light shining out of the tunnel you just left. They're almost here. Come on!" My muscles tensed. My voice revealed my fear.

"Get ready to take this rope down when I hit bottom."

Alex's steady voice and calm actions ticked me off. *He doesn't get it. We'll have to defend ourselves against the kidnappers. They'll be here any second.*

"I'm ready." As I held the rope, I looked around for something we could use to defend ourselves. My light swept over my backpack. Lightning was missing. *Not now. We don't have time for this.* I looked into the cavern.

Something snagged my sock. Glancing down I saw Lightning tugging at my other sock.

"You're mighty peppy." I caught him without releasing the rope, pulling him tight to my chest. Lightning gave me a big slurpy lick on the chin.

"What is it with you dogs and licking people?" I faked disgust as I shook my head. "I'm glad you're fine. I was worried about you."

Lightning jumped down, watching me and cocking his head.

Alex hit the cavern floor next to me, releasing himself from the rope.

I jerked hard on the rope a few times, causing it to come straight through the last C-ring at the top and fall to the cavern floor.

"That should keep those dummies from following us," Alex said. "See? No problem. We've just lost a few pitons, but we can get new ones." Alex reached for the rope on the ground.

A light from a flashlight reached the edge of the tunnel at the top of the cliff. The beam searched into the darkness.

"Forget the rope," I said. "There's no place to hide. We need to go that way." I pointed toward the path making its way through heaps of rocks up a slight incline. Lightning took off, followed by a slow-moving Thunder, then Alex and me. We scrambled on the trail around the jumbled rocks.

"Halt! Halt!" the Germans shouted after us. A flashlight nailed us in its beam.

Alex sprinted ahead. He stopped in twenty yards and swiveled around.

"Gabe, they're setting up a floodlight on the cliff face. And there are two ropes down the cliff. They'll rappel any minute. Run faster."

A searchlight burst into life, tracking our every move.

"Left," Alex said. I darted behind a boulder. The light followed.

"Split-up," I signed. Alex slipped further left, light tracking. I surged right, Lightning in tow. The searchlight stayed with Alex. I switched my headlamp off. Scrambled most of the way up the hill. Safe.

Thirty seconds later, lights around the cavern walls switched on, dimly illuminating the entire space, exposing Alex and me. I waved Alex up the hill.

"Almost made it work," he panted.

"There's got to be something we can do." I picked up some jagged rock pieces.

"Don't." Alex grabbed my arm. "Think. Focus."

I gulped back some tears.

"Let's finish going up the hill first." Alex pointed to the center of the cave. The dogs, now recuperated, shot away.

"Lightning and Thunder, get back here," I said when we reached the top of the small mound. I looked around.

The cavern was over four hundred yards across. We stood at the top of a slight rise in the center. The cavern wall on the other side had black holes of tunnel entrances. Ancient wooden doors either flanked or covered the holes. I could barely make out a path from each tunnel that snaked toward the top of the hill through shallow gullies, short ridges, and boulder rock formations. The paths led to the top of the hill, which was smooth ground.

"Amazing," Alex said as he rubbed his chin. "There are at least six tunnels on that side of the cave. It's a little confusing. Which way do we go?"

"I don't know," I swallowed hard, ignoring the empty pit in my stomach. "The light's still not strong enough to make out any details. We're too far away."

"We've got to decide right away." Alex exhaled hard as he readjusted his backpack and looked back toward the kidnappers. "Those guys are halfway down the cliff."

Focus. I told myself. *There has to be a way to know which tunnel is the right one.* Lightning caught my eye, sniffing at a short, foot-high carved rock post near the beginning of a path. He marked it as part of his territory and moved to another rock post at the beginning of another trail. Each post was like an eight-sided cylinder with a flat top. I dashed to the first post. The flat polished top had a symbol carved in it.

"Alex, look at this symbol. I bet it's a coat of arms. I don't know this one, but I do know the ones for Neuschwanstein and Hohenschwangau. Maybe there's a tunnel back to the castle."

"I remember the Neuschwanstein symbol, sort-of," Alex said. "Let's try to find it."

We rushed to different posts, intently staring at the symbols to find the one we needed. Alex went to the far right; I went to the far left. We worked our way back to the middle. Alex reached the middle and said, "There's nothing over here." Looking back at the cliff, he said, "And those guys are about to touch the ground."

"Alex," I shouted, "Here it is! Come here. The path is a little to the left, but almost straight across. See?" I pointed to the post. "That's the symbol of the coat of arms for Neuschwanstein."

"I'll take your word for it. Let's sprint." Alex glanced over his shoulder again.

With both our headlamps trained on the trail in front of us, we bolted across the cavern floor, followed by the dogs. The Neuschwanstein path wasn't as smooth as the first path we'd used. Stalagmites were taller here and surrounded the path. Broken, crushed stalagmites mixed with fist-sized stones covered the winding way, making for treacherous footing.

"Yeeow!" Rocks flying, I stumbled and fell. My left knee took the brunt of the fall. My hands slammed into the ground and slid forward as I stiffened my arms. My face stopped an inch from the jagged edge of a six-inch-high stalagmite, right off the path. *Be careful! Now get up and get moving.* I jumped to my feet, brushing away the dirt from my totally scraped knee as I tried to catch up to Alex.

Alex slowed when he was fifteen feet away from the entrance.

"Hey, pour it on," I said.

Alex ignored me for a few seconds as he looked behind him. "Those two guys are already at the top of the hill." Alex tensed his jaw. "One of them has a gun."

I turned. The taller man took aim. The double crack of his gun seemed louder than normal because of the echo. Dust flew into the air from a five-foot rock pile to the right of me. I jumped.

"Halt!" the men shouted. They ran down the hill toward us.

"Go!" I screamed with all my might as I almost fell into the wooden door at the cave entrance. I pulled on the handle of the door with all my might. No dice. I couldn't get in.

"They're too close," Alex said. "We're doomed."

Chapter 23

BATTLE ENGAGED

I made my hands stop shaking. *Get a grip on yourself!* I clawed for the black wrought iron handle, and yanked again. Nothing. I slammed my hand into the door, wincing as it hit a raised metal bar I hadn't seen. I jerked back, dragging my eyes away from the handle to scour the door. Two metal bars, one near the top and one near the bottom, ran from left to right through metal brackets bolted on the door and the rock wall.

Thunder slid near the door, spraying pieces of rock into me as he turned around. Barking with bared teeth, saliva spilling onto the ground, he raced back towards our pursuers with Lightning hot on his tail.

"Thunder and Lightning, come back here," Alex called.

"Alex, help me!" I dropped to my knees, straining to drag the lower bar to the left. Rusty and stiff, it resisted, but eventually gave way. Alex grunted, forcing the upper bar open. The dogs returned, still barking and growling at our attackers. I scrambled to the right, wrenched the door out a few feet, collared Lightning, and crammed him through the opening. Alex launched himself into the gap

151

and Thunder leaped over my bent form, nails from his hind paws scratching my neck. I tumbled inside and jerked the door shut, falling back on the floor.

Darkness swallowed our lights down the tunnel. My palms drove into the ground as I thrust myself into a sitting position and reversed direction. My light raked the backside of the door. Panting and ragged breathing punctured the momentary silence. The outside bars connected to parallel bars on the inside of the door. Alex and I collided as we rushed to struggle with the metal bars again.

"Can we lock the door?" Alex said after we slammed the bars home.

"There!" I said, pointing to the thick iron rod threaded through an upper and lower hinge attached to the two metal bars, connecting them from top to bottom. I threw the lock in place, jamming it into the metal-lined hole in the tunnel floor. Puffing hard, Alex and I pressed the sharpened rod as far down as it would go. Exhausted, I flopped back, sitting against the door and rubbing my neck where Thunder had scratched me. "Now we should be safe."

"For a little bit." Alex said, squatting next to his dog.

He's right. Heart pounding and muscles ready to explode, I forced myself to drink in details as my light slashed through the dark. Lightning jumped on my legs and licked my hand. *I'm glad you're here.* I grabbed him and held on tight while I looked around.

The cave was about eight feet high and twelve feet wide. The ceiling had light sockets at regular intervals hanging from a thick cable, but the bulbs were missing. I shifted my position, scraping my feet against broken stalagmites and rocks. The tunnel floor was level at first, but sloped downward after twenty feet. In the distance, there was a slight right-hand turn, then only darkness.

"I think we're headed under the Poellat Gorge," I said after a few gulps of air.

A slam against the door jolted me. The bolts and handle rattled. "Time's up," I said. Another thud shook the door.

"Run," Alex panted and stood up.

I squeezed Lightning and released him. Still winded, we took off. Both dogs zoomed in front. We sprinted all out, slowing for the slight right turn, our chests heaving as we blasted up a slight incline for at least the length of four football fields. The dogs dashed around a ninety-degree left turn.

"Wait," I gasped. A stalactite cracked overhead, breaking in pieces. A cloud of dust rose between Alex and me. The pointed end shattered inches in front of me and a heavy chunk grazed my left cheek, smacking my shoulder. I bent forward, hands on my knees, collapsing on one knee.

Alex whipped around. "Gabe, what's wrong?"

"Got hit from above. Stinger in my left arm."

"We'll slow down and keep watch overhead," Alex waved away the dust and came back. He dropped his backpack, pulled out a bottle, and gulped down water.

"I haven't heard them break in," I rubbed my shoulder, opening and closing my fingers to get back the feeling.

A distant deep beat kept up in the background. I looked ahead, my light picking out the dogs' eyes in the darkness. Both had returned from racing ahead, their tongues hanging out, rib cages heaving. Saliva dripped from the end of Thunder's tongue.

I struggled to my feet. "Bet it won't take them long to get through. I can't keep running that fast, but I can jog." Pulling out some water, I took a deep drink.

"Right," Alex said between breaths. "Jogging sounds good." He pushed himself off the wall, adjusted his headlamp, and looked down the tunnel. "I can't see the end. At least the tunnel hasn't gotten smaller." His shirt stuck to his sweaty back as he leaned over to stretch his legs. After a swig of water, he muscled his pack back into place. "Let's go."

"Ready." I stowed my water bottle. I wiped the sweat off my face, adjusted my headlamp and backpack, and settled into an easy pace.

As my light bounced around the black tunnel, I noticed less tan rock and more gray rock like the bottom part of Neuschwanstein. A few minutes later, the tunnel became a T intersection. At the intersection, the ceiling had sockets with light bulbs. The cable between the sockets looked tight and newer than the rest of the tunnel. To the right was a shallow, dead-end branch of the tunnel, with several large bags propped up against one corner. The left had no end in sight. I darted into the left tunnel and picked up the pace. Thirty feet into the tunnel, I found a short flight of concrete stairs that led up to a door recessed in the right wall. I dropped my backpack and lunged at the door. *Freedom!* I twisted, turned, pulled, and shook the doorknob with no success.

"Stupid door," I kicked it hard.

"Easy," Alex said.

"We're almost there," I said while pointing to the top of the door. "See the Neuschwanstein crest?" I pounded on the door with my palm and shouted, "Let us in!"

"No one's going to hear us this early in the morning," Alex said. He looked at his watch. "It's 4:30." He threw his pack on the ground and leaped two steps at a time to the door. "Let me try."

I stepped down and watched him do everything I had done.

"It's not working," he said. He quit jerking on the door handle and began to feel around the edges of the door while his light tracked along. "We've got to stop those guys behind us if they break through."

"How?" I said. My shoulders slumped. I jumped down a few stairs and plopped down.

"Thunder and Lightning," Alex said.

"Hmmm. Thunder and Lightning?" *Snarling growls, slashing teeth, bone-crunching jaws? Only Thunder is big enough to knock one of them over. But Lightning has blazing speed.* My mind zipped through defense tactics against the kidnappers.

"First, we've got to do something about that gun."

"Yep. He almost shot me back there." My dry tongue licked parched lips. I rubbed sweaty hands against my pants. I shoved myself off the stairs into a karate defensive stance.

"Karate won't work against a gun," Alex said. "We have to do something at long range."

Loose stones on the ground brought a ridiculous picture to mind. I stooped over, picked up some broken stones and slung them at the tunnel wall. I said in a horrible French accent, "I could toss a few pebbles at zem to see if zey would duck. I'm sure it will scare zem."

Alex's brief smile disappeared as he raised his eyebrows and looked down on me. "Always the clown, aren't you?"

I jumped up as another stray thought popped into my head. "Bingo! I almost forgot. I brought my sling. That should work." I snatched my pack off the floor, yanked a zippered pocket open, and snagged the sling. "Got it. Remember the sling contest last summer? Who took first place? That would be me, hitting the bulls-eye five out of seven times at fifty feet. Our headlamps light up stuff about a hundred feet away, giving me plenty of distance to fire away." My mind went into hyper-drive. *We may beat those kidnappers yet.* I stood and faced Alex. "I'll sling a rock at the gunman's head and I'll be like King David who killed Goliath. That'll stop him."

Alex widened his eyes, looked away and shook his head. "Where are your five smooth stones, little King David?" He sat down, put one elbow on a knee and thrust his head into the palm of his hand. He sucked in a deep breath and let it out. "Your plan doesn't make sense."

That made me mad. I glared at Alex and put a little venom in my voice. "And *you* have a better idea?"

Alex rubbed his head and leaned back, closing his eyes. After a second, he shrugged his shoulders. "I don't care. Do it your way. I don't think it'll work, but I can't think of anything better. But use Thunder and Lightning to harass and distract the bikers. I'll keep working on this door." Without waiting for a reply, Alex turned around.

"It'll work," I said. "I'm gonna find stones to use. They'll be sorry they hit me on the head! Come on, boys." I stormed down the tunnel with the two dogs as Alex worked on the door's handle and lock.

As I rounded the corner at the T-intersection, I heard distant thudding sounds. *They're too far away,* I told myself. *Quit imagining things.* Every few minutes I looked in the direction from which we had come, expecting the bikers to appear. No sign of them yet.

On hands and knees I scrambled around the long tunnel, raking among the gravel pieces with my hands trying to find smooth round stones, but finding only pebbles and large jagged rocks. Nothing. Frustrated, I stood and kicked some gravel into the wall, which raised a lot of dust and made the dogs jump back.

"Hey, boys, don't mind me." I called them back, squatted down, and let them lick my chin as I ruffled their necks and backs. "Let's make a plan."

Thunder and Lightning sat on their haunches, side by side, looking up at me as I stood. But when I spoke, they kept looking away. "Look at me," I said, but they looked either left or right, but not right at me. Thunder tried to cover his eyes with his paws.

"Oh, sorry guys," I laughed. "Is my light in your eyes?" I moved my headlamp to shine above their heads. I shook out my arms and stretched my neck to loosen up, then I laid out what I wanted them to do, showing the dogs their parts and using key words.

"When I *throw* the rock from my sling, *run* toward the men." I made a throwing motion with my sling. Both dogs turned their heads to follow the action, then swiveled back to me. "Thunder, *protect* us. You have to be the biggest, meanest, baddest dog that gunman has ever met." I jumped in the air, landed in a crouch with bunched shoulder muscles, and showed my teeth with a growl to add emphasis.

Thunder's tail thumped the floor of the cavern, knocking stones and dirt everywhere. He snarled, baring long white fangs.

Lightning pranced back and forth, his tail swishing the air.

"Lightning, *attack* them. *Run* fast, *bite* their ankles and make them chase you." Crouched down on my hands, I ran in circles, slashing the air with my teeth, then leaped away. "Do you get it?"

Lightning's ears pricked up. He jumped into the air, turned several rapid circles, and let out a piercing "Yip!" three times.

I smiled. They knew what to do. *Now we're almost ready.* I tugged my headlamp back into position and ran back to the T-intersection, stepping around the corner toward the door and whipping my backpack off my shoulders. I grabbed several short pieces of rope out of the pack and stuffed them under my belt. Ready for action, I looked up and saw Alex sitting on the last step in his thinker's pose, right elbow on his knee and chin on his fist, talking to himself. I could faintly hear what he was saying.

"I need leverage, like a crowbar, but ... I've got it." Alex shot over to his backpack and started rifling through the bag.

I bet he'll use rock-climbing maintenance tools. He never goes caving without them. The door was relatively modern, not old like the wooden one at the end of the tunnel. And this lock was newer, harder to pick than the key lock on the iron gate in the "lion's den." Distant sounds of German captured my attention. I gulped, shouldered my backpack, turned off my light, and snuck a look around the bend. Lights bobbed and weaved as the men approached. They were gaining ground rapidly. I switched my light back on and whispered, "Thunder and Lightning, here we go."

We dashed across into the dead-end tunnel branch on the other side. My feet slid out from under me. I slammed down on my side. Rocks, stones, and gravel cut deep. Sucking air, I rolled and knocked over a burlap bag. As I wrenched myself to my knees, my fingers sank into the spilled bag.

"Awesome," I said. My headlamp revealed round smooth stones perfect for my sling. *Thanks, God!* I snatched up five stones each about the size of a robin's egg. I jammed four of them into my pocket and loaded the fifth stone in my sling. I practiced swinging the sling in the dead-end alcove. It worked. I took some deep breaths to steady myself. *Accuracy is more important than speed. Make the first stone count.*

Light off, I spied around the corner, focusing on my aiming point. The two flashlights bobbing up and down rushed closer. Half-a-football-field away, shadowy shapes appeared. I pulled back and braced myself. Headlamp on, I thrust my head low into the tunnel. The taller biker jabbed his finger at me, shouting in German. The men raced closer. A hundred feet. *Steady.* Eighty feet. The gun glinted in the taller man's hands. I sprang to the center of the dead-end tunnel, steeled myself, and twirled the sling over my head.

Wait ... Now!

The first rock flew. The stone missed my target, but smashed the tall man's gun hand with incredible force. The gun clattered to the ground. He clutched his hand and howled with pain. I hollered with all my might, "Go, Thunder, sic 'em."

Like a midnight marauder, Thunder shot out into the dim light. His jet-black form covered sixty feet in less than twenty seconds.

I looked at Lightning next. *"Attack! Go! Go!"*

Lightning, much faster than Thunder, sliced through the distance in fifteen seconds, like an orange-red ball of fire in the dim light. The dogs reached their destination at the same time. His high-pitched yips echoing in the tunnel, Lightning ran through the shorter man's legs and turned left. Using his speed and the wall, he ran up the wall and bounced into the man's face. The man's grasping fingers found empty air, then clamped down on the furry adversary. Seizing the longhaired, barking rag mop by the hair, the black-haired man threw Lightning at the ground.

Lightning swiveled his hips like a cat and landed on all four paws. Using his legs like springs, he recoiled from the ground right back off the wall, this time landing on the man's right arm and shooting toward his neck. The kidnapper stumbled backward, missing Lightning with his left hand. Lightning wrapped his entire body around the man's neck, with his tail covering the man's eyes and nose.

As Lightning's rapid attack unfolded, Thunder charged the taller, blond-haired man. The man swung his flashlight. Too late. They went down in a heap. The flashlight skittered to the side. Blondie and Thunder tussled in semi-darkness. Thunder's muzzle grabbed the man's jacket and shirt from behind his neck. Thunder pulled the clothes over the biker's head and locked his arms above his head. Blondie struggled. No good. Thunder had control, but just to make sure, he tugged the man's clothes tight every few seconds. Shouts, barking, and growling filled the air.

I slammed my fist into my hand. "Got 'em."

The dogs had the upper hand.

I spun right, looking down the tunnel. "Alex, hurry! They're here. Is it open yet?"

A pile of gear lay by his pack, but no Alex and no response. I began to panic. "Hey, Alex," I said louder. "Help!"

Alex's head appeared from the recessed doorway. "I can't help. It's still locked. Hold them off." He disappeared.

"Great," I muttered, "I'll have do it all by myself." My sweaty fingers snagged a second smooth rock. I didn't want to hit the dogs. I took a deep breath. Swinging the sling, I ran toward the second guy. About forty-five feet away, his flashlight danced in crazy patterns from Lightning's attacks.

The dark-haired man in blue coveralls sneezed. He snapped up Lightning and heaved him to the ground. Lightning rolled right, then ran circles around the man's feet. The hoodlum bent over, swatting at Lightning. Lightning darted away. He jumped up on the biker's back, nipping his ears. The biker stood up. Waved his arms to get him off, shouting and beating the air.

Blondie cursed as Thunder dragged him in short bursts towards one of the tunnel walls. As he thrashed around on the ground, his clothing twisted tighter around his neck, leaving his head barely visible. His writhing took him closer to the gun lying on the ground, but Thunder kept dragging him away.

"Lightning, down," I yelled before letting the second stone rip. Lightning leaped to the ground.

The stone slammed into the dark-haired biker's right elbow. His flashlight tumbled out of his grasp and rattled on the stony floor. His left hand pressed hard on the elbow. He howled in pain. Lightning gave him no break, harassing him by nipping at his ankles and legs.

Without a sound, I charged down the tunnel and locked on the gunman. I had to pass the dark-haired guy, now intent on kicking Lightning, all the while bent over and holding his right elbow. After I got past him, I pointed and said, "Thunder, put Blondie against the wall."

Thunder dragged the man close to a wall, then with a sharp jerk of his neck, rolled his face and chest tight against the wall. In the process, some taller stalagmites sticking up from the floor scraped the kidnapper's chest and belly. His knees jerked up and he cried out in pain.

"Thunder, guard," I commanded.

Thunder's ferocious growl froze the gunman for the moment.

I leaned in close. "The dog will do whatever I tell him. No sudden moves." I slid him from the wall, kicked his knees away from his chest, and rolled him onto his stomach.

"Thunder, keep it tight." I jammed Blondie's right wrist into his jaws. I twisted his left arm behind his back. The gunman lay motionless. I whipped a rope around his left wrist and wedged my knee into a blocking position on the left arm. I took hold of his right wrist. As I brought down his right arm, he tried to wrench his left arm free, but I easily twisted his left arm up toward the back of his skull.

The man cried out.

I missed the swinging right arm. But Thunder didn't. Whirlwind reflexes brought control. The man's pained voice echoed in the tunnel. Riding on the biker like a bucking bronco, I said right next to his ear, "Stop moving or I'll break your arm." I jerked his left arm higher.

The man grunted, put his face on the gravel, and stopped struggling. I snatched his right wrist, twisted his arm, and swiftly tied his wrists together.

Thunder barked near the man's right ear, making his body twitch as if he'd been shocked. The man went limp, breathing in gasps. His eyes stayed shut, but he winced as I moved him. I tied his ankles tightly together. Then I pulled his wrists and ankles together behind his back with another rope. "Now you know how this feels." I tugged on the rope as hard as possible. As I worked on the last knot, I lost control. A hand like a vise gripped my hair and ripped me off the gunman.

Chapter 29

THE OPEN DOOR

As I fell backward, I twisted my head to see the attacker. Thunder lunged past me, barking and snapping at the man. I shifted right. Palms on gravel and knees underneath me, my face still grazed the ground. Lightning leaped toward the top of my head.

"*Schmerzen!*" the man shouted in pain as he let go of my hair to shake Lightning off his right hand. He kicked Thunder in the side.

The kick pushed Thunder sideways, but he recovered, reversing directions. He ignored the dark-haired man. His target now was Blondie, who wiggled toward the gun. Snarling, he hauled the man in the opposite direction.

Lightning hung onto the hair-grabbing biker's hand, using his hind legs to fight the crook.

For a split second, I locked up. *Blondie or dark hair?* Thunder's barking jolted me into action. I dashed to Blondie and finished the last knot. "Thunder, if he moves, bite him."

Thunder growled, raised his hackles, and showed his marvelous white teeth to the groaning gunman. The gunman stayed put.

I spun around. The dark-haired man had shaken Lightning off his hand and had run toward the gun. "Thunder, Lightning, sic him."

Before the dark-haired man gained control of the gun, Lightning leaped and latched onto his right hand again. He raised the black pistol with his left hand to smash Lightning, but he never completed the blow. Thunder launched into the biker's gut, knocking him into the wall. He grunted, toppling face forward as the gun skittered ten feet away.

Thunder circled the crook, growling.

I raced to the dazed biker's side. "Don't move!"

Thunder bared his teeth in the man's face.

I drove his chest into the ground, forced my knee into his back and curled his burly arms behind him. Face sideways, a short moan came from his lips. A bloody knot formed on his temple. *Must have cracked his head on the rock wall as he fell.* He gave weak resistance. His leg and arm movements were slow and he made a feeble effort to buck me off, but failed. He collapsed, unconscious.

Deft hand movements made quick work of tying him up as he had me. One rope was too short to tie both wrists together. *Stupid ropes.* I improvised, using a second rope to finish the job. I tied his ankles together, then strained to draw the ankles and wrists together with a connecting rope. Tired, I staggered to my feet to check my work.

Lightning trotted between the two men, tail held high, nose pointed into the air. He sniffed at each man, barked, and strutted away. It didn't wake the dark-haired man.

"Shut your trap," Blondie spit out, wiggling away.

Lightning ran back down the tunnel toward Alex. Thunder remained closer to the dark-haired man, nudging him to see if he would move.

I walked over to where Blondie lay against the wall. Red gashes and scratches covered his belly and back. His shooting hand had swollen from the stone's blow from my sling. The ropes held him tight. He swore at me when I touched him.

Satisfied, I left him and returned to the shorter, dark-haired man. Thunder dragged him ten feet away to the opposite wall. He seemed to stir as I inspected his bloody head. Scratches covered his square face and thick neck from the skirmishes with Thunder and Lightning. His right hand dripped blood from torn flesh.

"Thunder, guard them both," I said.

Thunder strutted back and forth between the two men, sniffing them.

"He'll attack if you move or try to escape," I told them both. I looked towards the Neuschwanstein door and took a deep breath. *Whew. Now that these guys are tied up, we should be home free.*

Lightning's barks filled the tunnel as Alex's light washed over him at the bend. Alex crouched down, rubbed his head, and flashed his light at me.

"Looks like Lightning has good news," Alex said in a loud voice. He smiled and hurried toward me. "I have good news too. I got the big door open."

"Awesome. These guys won't cause any more trouble." I rolled the black-haired kidnapper onto his right side toward Alex, exposing his tied up feet and arms. Then I leaned over him to show off my great rope tying skills. "See?" I glanced up. "I've got them both ..."

My voice suddenly choked off. I dropped to my knees, hands clawing at the hand thrusting up, squeezing my throat. I couldn't breathe.

"Let go," Alex hollered.

I couldn't break the iron grip on my throat. My eyes bulged. The ringing in my ears increased.

The man rocked more onto his back, his left hand still clutching my throat.

I beat on his broad chest, rock-hard stomach, and sides, but he squeezed harder. My eyes got blurry. Thunder's shadowy shape appeared, then disappeared. His hot breath hit my face as he clamped onto the biker's forearm.

"Yeee ... ah!" The man's agonized cry pierced through my fog, but his stranglehold didn't relax.

Time slowed. I felt weak and tried to focus. I'd failed. My thoughts frayed and sleep seemed inviting. Consciousness faded.

"I said, let him go." A fuzzy version of Alex's voice entered my dream.

Suddenly the pressure around my neck disappeared. I fell onto the man and then rolled off, choking and massaging my throat.

Alex wrenched the man away, using a German neckerchief to strangle him into submission.

Coughing through dust-filled air, I crawled to the wall and kept my eyes glued on the dark-haired man.

Alex rolled the biker onto his stomach. His legs and left arm were still tied. Alex twisted the right wrist up toward the back of his head. "Lay still." His captive squirmed, writhing in pain as Alex applied more pressure to the arm. The dark-haired man eventually stopped moving.

"Thunder, guard!" Alex commanded.

Thunder put his muzzle next to the man's nose. He drew back his lips, opened his jaws, and rumbled.

"You move again," Alex said, grabbing the biker's hair, shaking his head and forcing it back into Thunder's breath, "and I'll have my dog rip off your ear. Understood?"

"Unngh," was the man's reply.

Arms shaking, I moved on hands and knees to Alex and sat down. I tugged a spare rope out of my belt and tossed it to Alex.

With sure hands, Alex completed tying the man's right wrist to the left, and then to the rope connecting the wrists to the ankles. With the rope tightened, the biker's skin turned red. Alex flipped a frayed rope over to me. "Guess this one isn't good anymore. It's a good thing you used two ropes on this guy's wrists." He stood up and looked my way. "You haven't budged. You okay?"

"Okay," I said, my voice still harsh from being choked. I looked at the rope and swallowed. "I guess that guy had a sharp edge somewhere to cut the rope."

Alex dropped to one knee. "Found it." He smiled with satisfaction as he threw a blue leather belt to me.

I ran my hands over the belt. The back had a metal piece, two inches long in the center. From the top a sharp knife-edge stuck out far enough to cut the cord. The blade retracted by pushing a button on the side of the metal covering. "Pretty tricky," I said. "Let's check to see if he has anything else hidden in his clothes."

Alex searched the black-haired man, his fingers working from the neck down his blue jumpsuit, patting the back, waist, and between his legs. He pulled off the man's shoes and threw them in the direction of the large cavern.

"Why'd you do that?" I glanced his way.

"Ever try to walk in stocking feet in a cave?" He kicked some gravel at me.

"Ah, I get it." I searched Blondie the same way, ripping his boots off. I heaved one toward the cavern and one toward the castle entrance. "That's even better. If he gets loose, he'd only have one boot on for a while." I rubbed my throat, stepped over to Alex, and slapped him on the shoulder. "Thanks."

"No sweat," he said. "Where's the gun?"

My headlamp shot past the crook in the blue jumpsuit. Several feet away, a black handgun lay on the ground. I picked up the gun as a detective would in a movie, using the German neckerchief to hold the trigger guard. Satisfied the men couldn't get loose and that Thunder and Lightning would keep them from escaping, we hiked toward the T-intersection.

When we got to the turn, Alex stopped. "Like I was saying, the big door is open to the castle. Actually, there are three doors. I picked the lock on the first door, then worked some controls to open the third door at the end of a small room. That door leads directly into Neuschwanstein's kitchen. Unfortunately, there is an iron grate door in between the two bigger doors with square openings about 9 inches. There aren't any controls to open it and I can't figure out how it's locked. I think we found your secret passage."

We walked to the open doorway. I picked up my backpack and stuffed the gun in an outside pocket, zipping it closed and tossing the neckerchief next to the bag.

"I knew there was something to that engineer's map." I leaned against the wall. "Did you find a light switch?"

"No. I searched all around the door, but nothing."

"What's next?"

"We need to send for help." Alex shined his headlamp on his watch. "And we've got to watch these crooks. It's about 5:45 A.M. I bet there's a search party out looking for us."

"I can write a note. Lightning should be able to squeeze through the iron grate door. We can tie the note to Lightning's dog collar and send him out. He'll know where to go."

"Okay," Alex said as he twisted sideways to get a glimpse of the crooks. "Thunder can guard these biker-dudes while we wait. They could pull some other trick."

"All right." I sat down, scribbling with a pencil in a notebook from my backpack.

> Help! We're in Neuschwanstein castle,
> at the secret tunnel in the kitchen.
> Send police right away.
> We caught the bad guys.
> Gabe and Alex Zanadu

"Lightning, come here," I said. My whistle sounded like a shrill siren as I called my dog. Speeding through the dusty air, Lightning bounced into my arms. I wrapped the note in Alex's neckerchief, set the little dog on the ground and twisted the cloth under his collar, tugging it tightly into a square knot. "Lightning," I crouched down and held his muzzle in my hands, "Go to Mom and Dad in the parking lot. Got it?"

A single yip signaled "yes." He danced around my legs three times, climbed through a square in the middle door and shot away like greased lightning, his golden-red hair streaming behind him.

Behind me, Thunder barked in rapid bursts. The Germans' voices got louder, with Blondie bellowing at full volume. I raced with Alex to see what was wrong.

Chapter 25

GUARD DUTY

We arrived to see the kidnappers had moved together, back to back, trying to untie each other's hands. Thunder had latched onto the tall guy's jacket and dragged him away twisting, turning, and kicking. He let loose a stream of colorful words. The part in English was threats and foul language.

"We need to separate them more," I said.

"Yeah, and watch them every second," Alex said.

"Let's lug the shorter guy toward the door. We can sit between them and Thunder can go back and forth." I moved toward the dark-haired biker.

"Okay. Let's shine their lights on them, too. I want to make sure they don't try anything funny." Alex nabbed one light, set it on the tunnel side opposite Blondie, and adjusted the light to shine in his eyes. Then he got on the left side of the stocky man with me on the right. We hooked our arms under his shoulders and wrestled him ten feet closer to the exit.

"A little more," I said. I didn't want either kidnapper close to me.

The man kept wiggling his shoulders, pushing his body against our legs as we tugged him along. We repositioned ourselves. In spurts, we heaved and grunted, and dragged him another ten feet away.

"Enough," Alex said. He set the second flashlight on the dark-haired man.

Arms hanging, I trudged back to a point halfway between the two crooks. I sat, propped my elbows on my knees and let my face sink into my cupped hands. I rubbed my face and forced my eyelids to stay open.

"Don't fall asleep," Alex said as he sat opposite me.

"I'm not going to fall asleep. I'm just resting my eyes. I'm tired."

"We need to watch these guys until someone finds us."

"I *got* it. Give me a break." I looked both ways to make sure the bad guys were behaving. Neither had moved much since we dragged them apart. Thunder trotted from one man to the other. *They're not going anywhere. Thunder's a great watchdog. He'll bark if there's trouble.* I ached all over. My headache had come back. Thunder patrolled back and forth again and again. My head went back into my hands. My eyelids dropped. I fought to keep them from sliding shut. Each second seemed like a minute, each minute an hour.

A punch on the shoulder jolted me to my senses. I sprang into a crouch.

"Gabe," Alex said. He had crossed the tunnel to my side.

"What?" I focused my eyes on him.

"You fell asleep. We need to stay awake."

"I'm drained. I need sleep. Let's take turns."

"It's hard for me to stay awake, too. We have to move around or we'll both nod off." Alex hooked his thumb at one of the crooks. "That's what these two guys want."

"Okay," I said. I straightened and stretched, glancing toward the exit.

Without warning, a screeching, scraping sound like rusty hinges cut through the silence. The overhead lights in the short tunnel section containing the castle entrance flickered to life. The warm glow broke into the dreariness of the longer tunnel where we watched the kidnappers fifty feet away from the intersection of the two tunnels.

"Hello, anyone there?"

"That's Dad!" Alex grabbed my arm.

"Dad, we're down here," I cupped my hands to form a megaphone. "We're guarding the prisoners."

Five seconds later, Lightning dashed around the corner, down the tunnel, and jumped into my waiting arms.

"Hey, champ," I said, hugging him. "Glad you're back."

As Dad appeared at the corner, Alex sprinted toward him. "We're all right." He pointed in my direction. "There are the two men who kidnapped us." The policemen with Dad had turned on their flashlights to see better in the dim light.

Dad gave Alex a big hug, then headed over to me with a smile on his face. Looking at both crooks, he nodded. "Well done, you two. Well done." He gave me a great big bear hug that almost squeezed the air out of my lungs.

"See what we've done," I told him. "We used some of our climbing rope to tie their hands and feet. There's a rope—"

An older cop interrupted my conversation with Dad. "Ja, ja. We know some of this story." He looked around the cave where we stood.

I picked up my backpack and opened a pocket. When I offered the gun to the cop, he had another guy put it in a plastic bag. He took his time walking over to look at the captured crooks.

The rest of the Polizei followed him, taking care not to disturb the scene. *What will they think?* I asked myself, hoping we wouldn't be in any trouble because the attackers were scratched up pretty badly. One policeman made notes as another turned over each beat-up captive, pointing at the scratches all over their faces, hands, and bodies. The kidnappers didn't resist or say a word.

A lanky policeman left as the other nodded and turned back toward us. "We must take photographs, so we wait. My partner returns with camera," he said in broken English. He motioned to the criminals, "Why do they not have shoes on?"

" 'Cause it's hard for the crooks to walk in socks with floors like these," I said.

"Great thinking." The policeman scratched his head. "I have never seen this before."

Dad listened to Alex and I describe how we got free until the tall policeman returned and took pictures at various angles. The two criminals scowled at him as he completed his task. The guy in charge walked over and talked with Dad.

"We must have both boys and parents come to the Polizei station to answer a few questions," the officer said. "The dogs will have to stay outside. My men will take care of these two criminals."

I looked at my watch: 6:57. We walked up the stairs, through the first door, past the opened iron grate door into a six-foot-long space. On the right were shallow wooden cabinets three feet high. One was open and had several switches inside. *Probably the light switch and lock for the iron grate door is in there.* We kept going through the third door into the dazzling sunlight of Neuschwanstein's kitchen.

When we walked into the kitchen, I pulled Alex aside to look at the secret entryway. The disguised door in the kitchen swung into the tunnel. When closed, pots, pans, cutlery, and other kitchen tools hung on the door as though it was a solid wooden wall. Two-inch strips of white wood molding nailed to the outline of the door extended an inch over the door opening on every side. It looked like a picture frame for the pans and pots. The molding created a snug fit against the wall when closed, showing no gaps. Satisfied that I understood why we had missed seeing the door during the castle tour, I turned, took a few steps, and spotted Mom talking to a man in uniform.

"Mom!" I raced to meet her as she ran towards us.

"Gabe, Alex, you're safe." Her eyes were red and face a little whiter than normal. She gave me a huge hug, kissing me on the head, then held me at arm's length. "You look terrible. A mess." Wiping the glistening tracks of teardrops from her face, she grabbed Alex as he came up and wrapped her arms around him. She checked us out from top to bottom, front and back, protesting every time she saw a scratch, cut, or bruise.

After a couple of minutes, Alex spoke up. "Mom, we have to go to the Polizei Station. They need to take pictures of us and ask a few questions."

"Yeah," I chimed in. "We can't get cleaned up yet."

"Boys, we have a lot to talk about," Dad said as he came up behind us. "This has been quite an adventure, but your mother and I had a rough night, worrying and losing sleep. We'll need to get all the details from you and the police. Then we can discuss how we need to deal with your actions. You'll need to explain why you didn't follow my directions. Thank the Lord you only have cuts and bruises." He hugged each of us again and we all followed the police out.

I raised my eyebrows, looked at Alex, and shrugged my shoulders. *Where's the slap on the back for catching the crooks?* I swallowed hard. My initial happiness drained away. *Wonder what consequences we'll get for this? Probably pretty tough, considering we got ourselves kidnapped.*

The officer-in-charge motioned for all of us to follow him out of the kitchen and down the stairs to the castle exit. We piled into his car and he ferried us to our van. When the van was ready to move, we followed the Polizei car into Fussen to the police station.

"Dad," I said while stifling a yawn, "why didn't you come back to the cave entrance right away? Did something go wrong?"

"No, but everything took longer than I expected." He looked at me in the rearview mirror. "Fifteen minutes after I left you by the cave, I arrived at the parking lot. Your mother was talking to a Polizei officer about the van break-in. When she mentioned the motorcycles, I interrupted. Explained what we had been doing. When I mentioned a cave, the policeman pulled his head back and raised his eyebrows like I was lying."

"Lying?" Alex said.

Mom turned around and smiled. "He said all this in rapid-fire English. He looked all messed up with his sweaty concert clothes and hair falling into his eyes. He was puffing from running so hard. It all made him seem a little odd."

"Anyway, the Polizei officer said there wasn't a cave in the Poellat Gorge," Dad continued. "He said there weren't enough policemen on site to search a cave in the gorge and investigate the break-in at the same time. I argued with him, but he wouldn't budge. He looked up the two motorcycle license plates. Someone stole the bikes two days ago. After twenty-five minutes, I realized another half hour would be gone before I could get him to come to the gorge. I told your mother and the officer in charge that I'd get you and the dogs and come back down." He stopped talking as he avoided a car that cut in front of him.

"How long were you gone?" I asked.

"Over fifty minutes," Dad said. "When I reached the spot where I left you, there was no one there. And no sign of a cave entrance."

"That's because—"

"Let me finish, Gabe. You'll get to tell your story in a minute at the police station."

"Okay." I plopped my head into my hands and stuck out my lower lip.

"I figured you had been overpowered. I ran back down the hill, reported that you two were missing, and convinced the Polizei to walk up the gorge to search for you. When we didn't find you by midnight, the senior police officer sent us to the hotel. He stationed a three-man police team in the parking lot with instructions for one officer to check every half hour for sound and movement on the hill where you had disappeared. They also tried to find a 'black light' to look for the markings you left, but they couldn't find one. He promised to begin a full search at dawn."

We pulled into the parking lot at the Polizei station.

"Then what happened?" Alex asked.

Dad took off his seatbelt and turned around in his seat. "We spent a mostly sleepless night, praying nothing terrible had happened to you. The Schultz family prayed with us. I've never seen any of them that worried."

"We thought you might be gone for good," Mom said. Her voice wobbled and hands shook as she reached for her purse and pulled out a tissue. Huge tears welled up in her eyes and slid down her cheeks. She sniffled, shook her hair out of her face, then wiped away the tears and blew her nose.

Leaving Thunder and Lightning in the van on guard duty again, we went into the station. After an officer took several pictures, a male nurse gave Alex and me medical attention. Alex went first. Each of us had a head gash requiring three or four stitches to sew up. He cleaned up all of our scratches and scrapes and gave us aspirin for our headaches. The nurse told Mom how to care for our head dressings.

"Follow me," a policeman directed when the nurse said he was done. The cop led all of us to the office of Polizei Station Chief, Fritz Wangen. Chief Wangen shook our hands and invited us to sit down. After an hour of questioning, we left the station, heading away from Neuschwanstein and our hair-raising adventure.

I settled back into my seat with Lightning in my lap for the short ride to the hotel. When we passed the road that went to the Alpenblick and kept going straight, I sat up. "Mom. Dad. Where are we going? Our stuff's at the hotel."

Chapter 26

SUMMIT MEETING

I stretched my seatbelt forward to hear the answer to my question. *Why weren't we stopping at the Alpenblick?* Mom spoke first.

"You both need to sleep," she said. "We're going home."

"Boys," Dad said, "my leave's been cut short. When we were at the Polizei station in Fussen, I called my boss. Since we had found you, he wanted us to come back for security reasons; to keep us safe. He doesn't want us attacked again. I called Karl Schultz. They were still at the hotel. He agreed that his family would pick up the few things we had there and deliver them to us at home. We had already packed most everything in the van because we were going to the Salt Mines for the next part of our trip."

"The Schultz family has helped us a great deal on this trip. Pete and Jenna both went to get your stuff from the room," Mom added.

"I called the hotel and explained everything. They understood. My boss wants an update on the kidnapping. He said when I made sure you were home, safe and sound, to come in to work. I'll talk to you more about this tomorrow night. We've covered all the major points of your kidnapping since we found you. Since you haven't slept all night, it's time to get some rest. No more talking."

"Boys, the nurse told me you needed to be quiet and take it easy. Sleeping will help you recover." Mom handed us a snack. "Pull out a blanket and pillow from the back if you need to cover your eyes to sleep."

I was upset, but I accepted the food. I pressed my lips together and stiffened my body against the seat. There was no sense arguing; I'd get in trouble. *What about the rest of our vacation?* I forced myself to watch the scenery outside, munching on gorp.

Alex got out of his chair and pulled a few pillows and blankets out of the back. He got a drink and put it in my cup-holder and threw a blanket and pillow on top of me.

I shoved them on the floor. A few minutes later, my breathing slowed. I felt drained, completely wiped out. My eyes caught Thunder and Lightning collapsed on the van's floor, their strength sapped from the drugged meat and the all-night excitement. I finished my snack and drink. Wiggled around in the seat. Covering my head, I nestled in the pillow and fell asleep.

We got home about 4:00 P.M. Dad dropped us off with the bags at the house, then left for work. Mom gave us supper, made us unpack, take showers, and go to bed. When we got up mid-morning the next day, Dad had already left for work.

"Tonight after supper we're going to discuss what happened, but for now you're grounded," Mom said. "Your father's finding out more information from the Polizei. We need to get back to schoolwork."

She kept her word. We studied, but also did laundry, had recess time at the park, tended to Thunder and Lightning's needs, and made the meals.

Dad arrived home at his normal time for supper. He refused to talk about what he'd found out until later. *I bet we're gonna get it.* The wait made my stomach twist in knots. I didn't eat much supper.

With supper done, dishes cleaned up, and Thunder and Lightning fed, the family walked into Dad's office. Dad had arranged four wooden chairs in a small circle in front of his carved oak desk, leaving a space by two chairs for our dogs.

Dad smiled. "Let's have a seat."

Maybe this isn't going to be as bad as I thought.

Thunder and Lightning followed us into the room. Thunder flopped down by Alex's seat and Lightning jumped into my lap, stretching first before laying down with his eyes toward Mom and Dad. I stroked Lightning's hair to keep myself occupied.

"We have a lot to talk about," Dad said. "I'll try to make it quick. First, let's talk about what happened after I left you in the Poellat Gorge guarding the entrance of the cave." Looking first at Alex, then at me, he said, "I heard the whole story you told the Polizei. Is there anything else you want to say?"

"We're sorry. We messed up," Alex spoke up first, shifting in his chair.

My shoulders slumped a little. My head drooped. "Yeah, we were wrong," I agreed. "We didn't listen and we paid for it." My head came up. "But we both learned to trust each other a little more. I think by working together we got free instead of still being trapped with two crooks."

"You certainly did pay." Dad's comments stayed on the first half of what I said. "Would you do it again?"

"No way," I said as Alex shook his head.

"Okay," Dad said. "We forgive you. However, you're both grounded for three months for two reasons. One is to remind you of your mistake. The second is for training."

I creased my forehead and arched one eyebrow. *Did I hear that right?*

"I'm glad you both prayed for help in your situation. That was the right thing to do. I'm sure the Lord heard your prayers and protected you. But I want you more prepared for any future problems. I'm going to give you more training on defense, recognizing danger, and learning to solve mysteries."

I sat up straighter, bending forward and twisting Lightning's left ear.

"Your physical toughness, good problem-solving skills, and basic understanding of the Bible are a sound start. I'll help you build on that, but you'll have to work with friends to get sharp with practice. Now let me tell you what I found out over the past twenty-four hours."

As Dad got to his feet and picked up some papers from his desk, I let go of Lightning's ear and relaxed. *Training for the future? That's great. Maybe we can learn to use nunchucks!*

"Honey, you can fill me in later," Mom said, standing up. "I have some things to do in the kitchen." She kissed Dad, gave Alex and me a hug, and left the room.

Dad sat down and tilted his chair back on two legs. "Here's the story."

Chapter 27

FACT IS STRANGER THAN FICTION

"Your kidnappers are only part of the equation," Dad began. "Yesterday, I explained the kidnapping to my boss in great detail. Today, I visited the local Polizei Station Chief to find out what their investigation had uncovered."

"You talked with Mr. Bruno at the Station?" I jumped in. "My Volksmarch partner from last year?"

Dad smiled and dropped his chair back on the floor. He leaned forward. "Yes. He likes you two guys. He's proud of how you faced those kidnappers, escaped from them, and even captured them."

"We couldn't have done it without Thunder and Lightning." Alex hugged Thunder and patted his jet-black head.

"Bruno told me the older boy with the gun was a terrible shot," Dad chuckled.

"Terrible shot?" I looked at Alex. "We're lucky that guy wasn't any closer." I sat on the edge of my seat, both hands ruffling Lightning's hair. "Did you say the gunman was a boy?"

Dad nodded. "Those two young men were only seventeen and nineteen, even though they looked older." Dad looked at the

179

ceiling. "They're not the smartest kids around. The youngest left school to make 'spending' money. The older boy with the gun has a record for drug use—marijuana. He was only trying to scare you when he fired at you in the cave. He says the bullet came closer to you than he intended."

"Too close for comfort," Alex said, gripping the arms of his chair tightly.

"Yes, I agree," Dad said. Then he took a deep breath and adjusted his seat closer to us. He got up, flopped the papers he had been looking at on the desk, shut the door, and sat down again. "What I learned is highly sensitive, but I can give you some of the details. You can't tell any of your friends this part of our discussion. Understand?"

"Yes," we both said, nodding our heads.

Dad's knees were now twelve inches from us. His eyes narrowed a bit and he lowered his voice. "Your kidnapping, which we first thought was for human trafficking, has now been linked to an underground group called Machete. The group that attacked us is a small cell group that Machete controls." Dad paused. I moved a few inches closer and Dad kept going. "Chief Bruno says the Landespolizei, which is the State Police, have been working at infiltrating Machete for some time. The police's inside man confirmed the kidnappers worked for the mysterious third man we saw at the gasthaus restaurant. Your kidnapping was their test, to prove they were worthy to join Machete. One boy will spend time with a juvenile delinquent social worker for rehabilitation. The older one will be evaluated to determine if he will be tried as an adult. As a minimum, he will probably spend time in a juvenile delinquent prison for education and rehabilitation."

"Is there going to be a trial? Will we have to be witnesses?" Alex's back straightened and his eyes widened.

"Yeah, like those old lawyer TV shows?" I said. "We could tell everyone what really happened." I pointed my finger twice at the imaginary hoodlums in an imaginary courtroom. "You and you. Guilty as charged."

Dad planted one hand on my knee and one on Alex's. "The German police will handle this quietly. The German court system only allows closed trials for juvenile delinquents with the parents of the criminal, the accused, and the victim present. We'll have to attend a hearing, but not in a courtroom setting. And the police department doesn't want anyone to know this information yet. This incident has changed their current undercover investigation into Machete. Now they have to explore the entire tunnel system and use it to catch more criminals." Dad stood up again and walked behind his desk, looking out the window. Rubbing his jaw, he came around in front of the desk, sat on the edge, and sighed. "Here's the scary part. Machete cell groups contain dangerous men, far more dangerous than the two recruits you captured. Chief Bruno told me that once you are marked by an agency for kidnapping, it could happen again."

"But if they're an underground group, all we have to do is stay away from caves," I said. I shifted in my seat, dumping Lightning on the floor, and tucked my legs against the arm of the chair to face Dad.

"Underground doesn't mean in caves," Dad chuckled as he spoke. "It means they stay hidden. Now Machete is concerned about being discovered because we know about them. They probably won't bother us here in Goeppingen, but when we go on special trips, we need to be alert. That'll be part of your training."

"I have a question," I said.

"Yes?" Dad lifted his left eyebrow.

"Why didn't the Germans in Bavaria know about the cave and its connection with Neuschwanstein?"

"Good question." Dad made his way back to his chair next to us. "King Ludwig liked to be alone and wanted a mysterious way to disappear. He swore a family friend to secrecy. The friend was a construction engineer who brought in poor foreign workers to build a hidden tunnel under cover of darkness to connect the Hohenschwangau and Neuschwanstein castles. When they completed the project, the engineer paid them well to keep silent and sent them home. No one in the area knew of the project. However, the engineer misplaced one of his original drawings of the tunnel—the one you found in the German library. One goal of the cell group that kidnapped you was to retrieve the map so no one else would find the cave and tunnels. Before we left on vacation, the crooks overheard you talking about the map with some friends. At the Alpenblick, they broke into your room to get the map."

"That's why our door was open that first night," Alex said. "But if the tunnel was between the two castles, it doesn't make sense. We found the tunnel in the Poellat Gorge."

Dad stroked his chin with his left hand. "King Ludwig's mysterious and untimely death soon after the tunnel completion kept the existence of the passage unknown, since the engineer was under an oath not to reveal it to anyone. Within days of the king's death, the engineer had a 'fatal accident' at the hands of Machete's founders. Using the map, they found the tunnel and later discovered the large cavern. The big cave became the central connection point for all the other tunnels they built to conceal human trafficking, drug running, and other illegal activities."

"But how did we find the cave that easily?" I said. I changed position again, picking up Lightning and squirming back into place. "You and the Polizei searched in the dark for hours and couldn't find it."

"You're right," Dad said. "I'll get to that part in a second. These bumbling kidnappers had several plans working all at once to ensure they didn't fail at their mission. First, there was the threatening note at the castle. They probably wanted to take you at the Alpenblick when your mother and I went to the concert alone. Second, they opened the cave in the daytime and used a mirror to attract your attention. We're not sure why they didn't take you then. Maybe they weren't expecting the dogs. The third and final scheme was the van break-in to get us to chase them."

Dad stretched out his back. "Now, the reason the police couldn't find the cave is because the door to the cave entrance is made of rock that matches the rocky cliff face. It's heavy, rolls on hidden rubber tires in front of the opening you saw, slides into the cliff and looks like a normal rock outcropping when closed. The builders were very precise. And since the door slides in front of the opening, it hid the black-light markings you made around the entrance."

"Okay." Alex scratched his head. "But what about the kitchen entrance? How did that work?"

Dad relaxed back into his chair. "The Neuschwanstein kitchen door switch was hidden within a little bookshelf right next to the pots and pans. You pull a lever behind the *Schwangau Family Cookbook*. It unlatches the spring, allowing the door to swing into the tunnel entrance."

I glanced at Alex. "That's why Thunder and Lightning were sniffing by the bookcase during the tour."

Dad nodded.

"I still don't get it," I said. "If they already took the map of the tunnel connecting the two castles they wanted, why did they kidnap us?"

Dad motioned for us to come closer. He whispered, "Blackmail."

"What do you know that they could want?" I blurted out.

"It's an Army special project. I can't tell you anything else, but the project's the reason they slashed the tire on the van." Dad stood and patted both our shoulders. He smiled. "That's it."

"One last question, Dad," I said without hesitation. "Why did the phone in our gasthaus room ring the evening before we got kidnapped?"

"Oh, yes," he said, coaxing Alex and me out of our seats, then turning us to the door. "As I said, they weren't the brightest guys. They called to ensure you were out of the room. Obviously, there's no guarantee you're out of the room if you don't answer the phone. Their next brilliant idea was to stand under our balcony later that evening, to find out our activities for the next day. That didn't work, so they arranged for their boss to listen to you at breakfast in the morning. Total amateurs."

Alex opened the door. The dogs scooted through first and Dad steered us down the hall. "Remember, most of what we talked about is our secret. But now, I've got something I want to show you." He pushed us ahead of him into our large entryway, the Great Room.

"Surprise!" everyone shouted.

The Schultz family and Mr. Bruno laughed. Mom and Dad clapped their hands. My mouth opened and I turned towards Dad. Alex put his hands on his hips and looked at our friends.

"Surprise about what?" I asked Dad.

"You'll see," he said.

I shook my head and rambled over to Pete, punching him in the shoulder. "Hey, man, good to see you."

Alex didn't say anything at first, but walked over to Jenna. Pete and Jenna's parents stood on one side of the great hall next to a table covered with a dark blue paper tablecloth topped with a double chocolate cake, sodas, and balloons of every color. Dad gathered Alex and me together, stood us beside each other against the wall opposite the table, and had the dogs sit by our sides. While Jenna and her mom took pictures of everyone, Chief Bruno Barr puffed out his chest and picked up a tray with two small boxes on top. He handed the tray to Dad and they both stood facing us.

"Alex and Gabe, we're delighted you are safe," Chief Bruno said. "I have a medal for each of you to express the German Polizei Department's appreciation for your capture of the two kidnappers. *Dankeschön.*" He took the medals out of each box one at a time and placed them around our necks. He shook each of our hands, grinning from ear to ear and smiling for each picture.

"Let's get pictures for me too," Dad said as he followed Chief Bruno.

Mom leaned over to smother each of us with a hug.

Everyone cheered and clapped after the pictures.

"Time for cake," Mom said. "Boys, you're first."

As we lined up for our food, Dad announced, "The next vacation will be at the Salt Mines in Bad Reichenhall, where we originally planned to go after seeing the Neuschwanstein castle. We should finish the trip we started. Agreed?" Dad raised his eyebrows, tilted his head, and glanced at Karl and Frieda Schultz.

"Ja, ja," Karl responded in a bass voice. "Certainly we will vacation together with you. We must visit the Salt Mines together."

I talked with Pete for a while, telling him some of what Dad had said. After thirty minutes, they all had to leave. We cleaned up and I put out water and a snack for the dogs. My body tingled all over. I knew I'd be awake for a while. I rubbed my hands over the medal on my chest and wandered over to the dining room to look out the front window. A single lamp lit our street corner, which was a crossroads. The main traffic flow came at our apartment building from the right and had to turn left at the intersection. The street to the front of our second floor apartment was a side avenue with almost no traffic at this time of night. The ancient lamppost's weak light cast faint shadows on the sidewalks.

A blur of movement caught my eye. A thin, medium-sized figure clothed in black darted into a recessed doorway to my left. I plastered my face against the window to see him. Staying in the shadows, the figure dashed to the covered entryway of the music store across the street from our apartment. The mysterious stranger carried a bulky brown paper package. He wore a dark stocking cap pulled low over his eyes and a black leather jacket with collar zipped up to his grayish beard. His pants, gloves, and shoes were all dark. He seemed nervous as he poked his head out of the entryway, looking left then right. He scampered to our outside door, disappearing from sight. The doorbell rang and the figure raced back the way it had come.

"I'll get it," I said, rushing around the table into the Great Hall to reach our inside door first. I ripped the door open and Thunder and Lightning nosed their way in front of me onto the upstairs landing. I took the stairs two at a time, following their wagging tails. I twisted the door handle and stuck my face out into the night air, beating the dogs back with my arm. "No, we're not going out. Get back."

They listened and moved back. Lightning danced around and Thunder stood at the ready, head cocked to one side, mouth wide open and tongue hanging out.

I turned my attention back to the package outside the door. I bent down to check it out. Plain light-brown paper covered the two-foot high, one-foot-by-one-foot object. The paper was blank, but taped to the side was a short note.

> **Alex and Gabe,**
> **Six months and counting.**
> **Team Test #2**
> **Survival kit enclosed.**
> **G**

I checked up and down the street, but the stranger was gone. I got down on my knees and looked under the package, but it was too dark to see anything. Snatching it up, I bounded upstairs with the dogs, brain churning. *Survive what?*

MORE
THUNDER AND LIGHTNING
BOOKS
COMING SOON!

Book Two

The
SALT MINES MYSTERY

Future books

The boys and their four-legged friends will travel to Austria; Germany; Okinawa, Japan; Hawaii; and Texas and discover endless mysteries and clues.

Meet Author Aaron Zook

Aaron M. Zook, Jr., a retired U.S. Army Colonel, shares his love for life through Christian books and songs. Aaron's Thunder and Lightning book series takes two adventurous boys and their talented canine sidekicks into mystery and intrigue. Through each medium, Aaron opens windows of insight into God's work in His creation. Enjoy God's laughter in simple pleasures. Relax in His cleansing light while dealing with earthly issues and relationships.

Sign up for THE ZOOK BOOKS newsletter at www. zookbooks.org

Made in the USA
Columbia, SC
29 October 2017